The same clanging noise that had called everyone in from the front lawn blared again. It seemed to come from right above Katy's head.

She cringed, wishing she could drop her backpack and cover her ears. "What *is* that?"

Shelby gawked at her as if she'd suddenly sprouted green ears and a tail. "That's the *class bell*. That's how we know it's time to go to the *next class*."

"Bell?" Katy shook her head, her ears still ringing from the horrible attack of noise. "Bells go ring-a-ling. That thing goes *braaawnk!*" The classroom door flew open and students spilled into the hall just in time to hear the awful sound leave her throat. Laughter rang, even more offensive than the so-called bell.

Katy asked one more question.

"Where is the ladies' room?"

Shelby pointed.

Katy turned and ran.

Katy's New World

Kim Vogel Sawyer

KATY LAMBRIGHT SERIES

ZONDERVAN®

ZONDERVAN.com/
AUTHORTRACKER
follow your favorite authors

C

ZONDERVAN

Katy's New World

Requests for information should be addressed to:

Zondervan, *Grand Rapids, Michigan 49530*

Library of Congress Cataloging-in-Publication Data

Sawyer, Kim Vogel.-
Katy's new world / by Kim Vogel Sawyer..
p. cm.—(Katy Lambright series ; bk. 1)
Summary: Katy Lambright gets permission to attend a public high school outside of her Mennonite community, but her relationships with her family and lifelong friends become strained as she struggles to find a balance between two very different worlds.
Includes bibliographical references.
ISBN 978-0-310-71924-3 (softcover)
1. Mennonites—Juvenile fiction. [1. Mennonites—Fiction. 2. Christian life—Fiction. 3. High schools—Fiction. 4. Schools—Fiction. 5. Friendship—Fiction. 6. Family life—Kansas—Fiction. 7. Kansas—Fiction.]
I. Title.
PZ7.S26832Kat 2010
[Fic]—dc221 2009032639

All Scripture quotations, unless otherwise indicated, are taken from *The Holy Bible, King James Version, KJV.*

Published in association with Hartline Agency, Pittsburgh, Pennsylvania 15235.

Cover design: Rule 29
Cover photography: Marc Raines
Interior design: Carlos Eluterio Estrada

Printed in the United States of America

---

10 11 12 13 14 15 /DCI/ 6 5 4 3 2 1

Dedicated to the many boys and girls
who entered my fifth grade classroom
at Morgan Elementary.

Thank you for challenging and enriching my life.

"To every thing there is a season,
and a time to every purpose under the heaven:
... A time to rend, and a time to sew ..."
Ecc. 3:1, 7a

Chapter One

Like wisps of smoke that upward flee,
Disappearing on the breeze,
Days dissolving one by one . . .
Time stands still for no one.

Katy Lambright stared at the neatly written lines in her journal and crinkled her brow so tightly her forehead hurt. She rubbed the knot between her eyebrows with her fingertip. What was wrong? Ah, yes. Two uses of "one" at the ends of the final lines. She stared harder, tapping her temple with the eraser end of her pencil. What would be a better ending?

She whispered, "Time's as fleeting as the— "

"Katy-girl?"

Just like the poem stated, her thought dissipated like a wisp of smoke. Dropping her pencil onto the journal page, she smacked the book closed and dashed to the top of the stairs. "What?"

Dad stood at the bottom with his hand on the square newel post, looking up. "It's seven fifteen. You'll miss your bus if we don't get going."

Katy's stomach turned a rapid somersault. Maybe she shouldn't have fixed those rich banana-pecan pancakes for breakfast. But she'd wanted Dad to have a special breakfast this morning. It was a big day for him. And for her. Mostly for her. "I'll be right down."

She grabbed her sweater from the peg behind her bedroom door. No doubt today would be like any other late-August day — unbearably hot — but the high school was air conditioned. She might get cold. So she quickly folded the made-by-Gramma sweater into a rough bundle and pushed it into the belly of the backpack waiting in the little nook at the head of the stairs.

The bold pink backpack presented a stark contrast to her simple sky blue dress. A smile tugged at the corners of her lips, while at the same time a twinge of uncertainty wiggled its way through her stomach. She'd never used a backpack before. Annika Gehring, her best friend since forever, had helped her pack it with notebooks and pencils and a brand-new protractor — all the things listed on the supply sheet from the high school in Salina. They had giggled while organizing the bag, making use of each of its many pockets.

Katy sighed. A part of her wished that Annika was coming to high school and part of her was glad to be going alone. If she made a fool of herself, no one from the Mennonite fellowship would be there to see. And as much as she loved Annika, whatever the girl saw she reported.

"Katy-girl!" Dad's voice carried from the yard through the open windows.

Would Dad ever drop that babyish nickname? If he called her Katy-girl in front of any of the high school kids, she'd die from embarrassment. "I'm coming!" She yanked up the backpack and pushed her arms through the straps. The backpack's tug on her shoulders felt strange and yet exhilarating. She ran down the stairs, the ribbons from her mesh headcovering fluttering against her neck and the backpack bouncing on her spine—one familiar feeling and one new feeling, all at once. The combination almost made her dizzy. She tossed the backpack onto the seat of her dad's blue pickup and climbed in beside it. As he pulled away from their dairy farm onto the dirt road that led to the highway, she rolled down the window. Dust billowed behind the tires, drifting into the cab. Katy coughed, but she hugged her backpack to her stomach and let the morning air hit her full in the face. She loved the smell of morning, before the day got so hot it melted away the fresh scent of dew.

The truck rumbled past the one-room schoolhouse where Katy had attended first through ninth grades. Given the early hour, no kids cluttered the schoolyard. But in her imagination she saw older kids pushing little kids on the swings, kids waiting for a turn on the warped teeter-totter, and Caleb Penner chasing the girls with a wiggly earthworm and making them scream. Caleb had chased her many times, waving an earthworm or a fat beetle. He'd never made her scream, though. Bugs didn't bother Katy. She only feared a few things. Like tornadoes. And people leaving and not coming back.

A sigh drifted from Dad's side of the seat. She turned to face him, noting his somber expression. Dad always looked serious. And tired. Running the dairy farm as well as a household without the help of a wife had aged him. For a moment guilt pricked at Katy's conscience. She was supposed to stay home and help her family, like all the other Old Order girls when they finished ninth grade.

But the familiar spiral of longing—to learn more, to see what existed outside the limited expanse of Schellberg—wound its way through her middle. Her fingernails bit into the palms of her hands as she clenched her fists. She *had* to go. This opportunity, granted to no one else in her little community, was too precious to squander.

"Dad?" She waited until he glanced at her. "Stop worrying."

His eyebrows shot up, meeting the brim of his billed cap. "I'm not worrying."

"Yes, you are. You've been worrying all morning. Worrying ever since the deacons said I could go." Katy understood his worry.

She'd heard the speculative whispers when the Mennonite fellowship learned that Katy had been granted permission to attend the high school in Salina: *"Will she be Kathleen's girl through and through?"* But she was determined to prove the worriers wrong. She *could* attend public school, *could* be with worldly people, and still maintain her faith. Hadn't she been the only girl at the community school to face Caleb's taunting bugs without flinching? She was *strong*.

She gave Dad's shoulder a teasing nudge with her fist. "I'll be all right, you know."

His lips twitched. "I'm not worried about you, Katy-girl."

He was lying, but Katy didn't argue. She never talked back to Dad. If she got upset with him, she wrote the words in her journal to get them out of her head, and then she tore the page into tiny bits and threw the pieces away. She'd started the practice shortly after she turned thirteen.

Before then, he'd never done anything wrong. Sometimes she wondered if he'd changed or she had, but it didn't matter much. She didn't like feeling upset with him — he was all she had — so she tried to get rid of her anger quickly.

They reached the highway, and Dad parked the pickup on the shoulder. He turned the key, and the engine spluttered before falling silent. Dad aimed his face out his side window, his elbow propped on the sill. Wind whistled through the open windows and birds trilled a morning song from one of the empty wheat fields that flanked the pickup. The sounds were familiar — a symphony of nature she'd heard since infancy — but today they carried a poignancy that put a lump in Katy's throat.

Why had she experienced such a strange reaction to wind and birds? She would explore it in her journal before she went to bed this evening. Words — *secretive whispers, melodious trill* — cluttered her mind. Maybe she'd write a poem about it too, if she wasn't too tired from her first day at school.

Cars crested the gentle rise in the black-topped highway and zinged by — sports cars and big SUVs, so different from the plain black or blue Mennonite pickups and sedans that filled the church lot on Sunday mornings in Schellberg. When would the big yellow bus appear? Katy had been warned it wouldn't be able to wait for her. Might it have come and gone already? Her stomach fluttered as fear took hold.

Dad suddenly whirled to face her. "Do you have your lunch money?"

She patted the small zipper pocket on the front of the backpack. "Right here." She hunched her shoulders and giggled. "It feels funny not to carry a lunch box." For as far back as she could remember, Katy had carried a lunch she'd packed for herself since she didn't have a mother to do it for her.

"Yes, but you heard the lady in the school office." Dad drummed his fingers on the steering wheel. "She said the kids at this school eat in the cafeteria or go out to eat."

Embarrassment crept over Katy as she remembered the day they'd visited the school. When the secretary told Dad about the school lunch program, he'd insisted on reading the lunch menu from beginning to end before agreeing to let his daughter eat "school-made food."

Truthfully, the menu had looked more enticing than her customary peanut butter sandwich, but Dad had acted as though he thought someone might try to poison her. She'd filled three pages, front and back, in her journal over the incident before tearing the well-scribbled pages into miniscule bits of litter. But—satisfaction welled—Dad had purchased a lunch ticket after all.

The wind tossed the satin ribbons dangling from the mesh cap that covered her heavy coil of hair. They tickled her chin. She hooked the ribbons in the neck of her dress and then brushed dust from the skirt of her homemade dress. An errant thought formed. *I'm glad I'll be eating cafeteria food like a regular high school kid. It might be the only way I don't stick out.*

Dad cleared his throat. "There she comes."

The school bus rolled toward them. The sun glared off the wide windshield, nearly hiding the monstrous vehicle from view. Katy threw her door open and stepped out, carrying the backpack on her hip as if it were one of her toddler cousins. She sucked in a breath of dismay when Dad met her at the hood of the pickup and reached for her hand.

"It's okay, Dad." She smiled at him even though her stomach suddenly felt as though it might return those banana-pecan pancakes at any minute. "I can get on okay."

The bus's wide rubber tires crunched on the gravel as it rolled to a stop at the intersection. Giggles carried from inside the bus when Dad walked Katy to the open door. Katy cringed, trying discreetly to pull her hand free, but Dad kept hold and gave the bus driver a serious look.

"This is my daughter, Katy Lambright."

"Kathleen Lambright," Katy corrected. Hadn't she told Dad she wanted to be Kathleen at the new school instead of the childish Katy? Dad wasn't in favor, and Katy knew why. She would let him continue to call her Katy—or Katy-girl, the nickname he'd given her before she was old enough to sit up—but to the Outside, she was Kathleen.

Dad frowned at the interruption, but he repeated, "Kathleen Lambright. She is attending Salina High North."

The driver, an older lady with soft white hair cut short and brushed back from her rosy face, looked a little bit like Gramma Ruthie around her eyes. But Gramma would never wear blue jeans or a bright yellow polka-dotted shirt. One side of the driver's mouth quirked up higher than the other when she smiled, giving her an impish look. "Well, come on aboard, Katy Kathleen Lambright. We have a schedule to keep."

Another titter swept through the bus. Dad leaned toward Katy, as if he planned to hug her good-bye. Katy ducked away and darted onto the bus. When she glanced back, she glimpsed the hurt in Dad's eyes, and guilt hit her hard. This day wasn't easy for him. She spun to dash back out and let him hug her after all, but the driver pulled a lever that closed the door, sealing her away from her father.

Suddenly the reality of what she was doing — leaving the security of her little community, her dad, and all that was familiar — washed over her, and for one brief moment she wanted to claw the doors open and dive into the refuge of Dad's arms, just as she used to do when she was little and frightened by a windstorm.

"Have a seat, Kathleen," the driver said.

Through the window, Katy watched Dad climb back into the pickup. His face looked so sad, her heart hurt. She felt a sting at the back of her nose — a sure sign that tears were coming. She sniffed hard.

"You've got to sit down, or we can't go." Impatience colored the driver's tone. She pushed her foot against the gas pedal, and the bus engine roared in eagerness. More giggles erupted from the kids on the bus.

"I'm sorry, ma'am." Katy quickly scanned the seats. Most of them were already filled with kids. The passengers all looked her up and down, some smirking, and some staring with their mouths hanging open. She could imagine them wondering what she was doing on their bus. She'd be the first Mennonite student to attend one of the Salina schools. She lifted her chin. *Well, they'll just have to get used to me.*

Katy ignored the gawks and searched faces. She had hoped to sit with someone her own age, but none of the kids looked to be more than twelve or thirteen. Finally she spotted an open seat toward the middle on the right. She dropped into it, sliding the backpack into the empty space beside her.

The bus jolted back onto the highway with a crunch of tires on gravel. The two little girls in the seat in front of Katy turned around and stared with round, wide eyes. Katy smiled, but they didn't smile back. So she raised her eyebrows high and waggled her tongue, the face she used to get her baby cousin Trent to stop crying. The little girls made the same face back, giggled, and turned forward again.

Throughout the bus, kids talked and laughed, at ease with each other. Katy sat alone, silent and invisible. The bus bounced worse than Dad's pickup, and her stomach felt queasier with each mile covered. She swallowed and swallowed to keep the banana-pecan pancakes in place. *Think about something else ...*

High school. Her heart fluttered. *Public* high school. A smile tugged on the corners of her lips. Classes like botany and music appreciation and literature. *Literature ...*

When she'd shown Annika the list of classes selected for her sophomore year at Salina High North, Annika had shaken her head and made a face. "They sound *hard*. Why do you want to study more anyway? You're weird, Katy."

Remembering her friend's words made her nose sting again. Annika had been Katy's best friend ever since the first grade when the teacher plunked them together on a little bench at the front of the schoolroom, but despite their lengthy and close friendship, Annika didn't understand Katy.

Katy stared out the window, biting her lower lip and

fighting an uncomfortable realization. Katy didn't understand herself. A ninth grade education seemed to satisfy everyone else in her community, so why wasn't it enough for her?

Why were questions always swirling through her brain? She could still hear her teacher's voice in her memory: "Katy, Katy, your many questions make me tired." Why did words mean so much to her? None of her Mennonite friends had to write their thoughts in a spiral-bound notebook to keep from exploding. Katy couldn't begin to explain why. And she knew, even without asking, that was what scared Dad the most. She shook her head, hugging her backpack to her thudding heart. He didn't need to be worried. She loved Dad, loved being a Mennonite girl, loved Schellberg and its wooden chapel of fellowship where she felt close to God and to her neighbors. Besides, the deacons had been very clear when they gave her permission to attend high school. If she picked up worldly habits, attending school would come to an abrupt and permanent end.

A prayer automatically winged through her heart: *God, guide me in this learning, but keep me humble. Help me remember what Dad read from Your Word last night during our prayer time: that a man profits nothing if he gains the world but loses his soul.*

The bus pulled in front of the tan brick building that she and Dad had visited two weeks earlier when they enrolled her in school. On that day, the campus had been empty except for a few cars and two men in blue uniforms standing in the shade of a tall pine tree, smoking cigarettes. Dad had hurried her right past them. Today, however, the parking lot overflowed with vehicles in a variety of colors, makes, and models. People—people her age, not like the kids on the school bus—stood in little groups all over the grassy yard, talking and laughing.

Katy stared out the window, her mouth dry. Most of the students had backpacks, but none sporting bold colors like hers. Their backpacks were Mennonite-approved colors: dark blue, green, and lots and lots of black. Should she have selected a plain-colored backpack? Aunt Rebecca had clicked her tongue at Katy's choice, but the pink one was so pretty, so different from her plain dresses ... Her hands started to shake.

"Kathleen?" The bus driver turned backward in her seat. "C'mon, honey, scoot on off. I got three more stops to make."

Katy quickly slipped her arms through the backpack's straps and scuttled off the bus. The door squealed shut behind her, and the bus pulled away with a growl and a thick cloud of strong-smelling smoke. Katy stood on the sidewalk, facing the school. She twisted a ribbon from her cap around her finger, wondering where she should go. The main building? That seemed a logical choice. She took one step forward but then froze, her skin prickling with awareness.

All across the yard, voices faded. Faces turned one by one—a field of faces—all aiming in her direction. She heard a shrill giggle—her own. Her response to nervousness.

Then, as suddenly as it had begun, the pull on the other kids faded. They turned back to their own groups as if she no longer existed. With a sigh, she resumed her progress toward the main building, turning sideways to ease between groups, sometimes bumping people with her backpack, mumbling apologies and flashing shy smiles. She'd worked her way halfway across the yard when an ear-piercing clang filled the air. The fine hairs on her arms prickled, and she stopped as suddenly as if she'd slammed into the solid brick wall of the school building.

The other kids all began moving, flinging their backpacks over one shoulder and pushing at one another. Katy got swept along with the throng, jostled and bumped like everyone else. Her racing heartbeat seemed to pound a message: *This is IT! This is IT!* High school!

Chapter Two

Just inside the wide double doors, a smiling woman held a big paper sign in the brightest pink Katy had ever seen. Pinker, even, than her backpack. In tall black letters, the sign directed new students to turn right at the first corner for "orientation."

Katy joggled her way to the right and followed several other kids around a corner, down a short hallway, to a room with another bold pink sign marked NEW STUDENT ORIENTATION. Although the word *orientation* was a new one, Katy vaguely remembered reading the word in the pamphlet the school had sent, and so she entered the room.

A man wearing a bright orange tie directed everyone to enter the room and "take a seat—any seat." Two long tables lined with chairs waited in the square room. Katy perched on the edge of a chair at the far end of the nearest table and placed her backpack on the floor beside her feet. She glanced at the others who'd entered the room and noticed that some of them appeared as perplexed as she felt. The thought gave her a small measure of reassurance.

The chairs filled quickly with students, and the man

with the funny tie snapped the door closed and bustled to the front of the room. He clapped his hands several times. "Quiet, please. Ladies, gentlemen, quiet now ..." The shuffling and mumbles slowly drifted away. When silence reigned, the man said, "Thank you. Good morning."

"Good morning," Katy replied automatically, then shrank back in embarrassment. At her school in Schellberg, each day had begun with Miss Yoder's greeting followed by the students replying in chorus. But none of the other kids in the room responded to the man's salutation, leaving her solo voice hanging in the air like an unpleasant odor.

Suddenly, from the other end of the table, a male student called, "Good morning," in a girlish, cheerful tone that perfectly matched Katy's. Several others snickered, and two more kids echoed the "Good morning." Katy hunched forward, trying to make herself smaller.

The man gave a firm shake of his head accompanied by a scowl, once again silencing the students. "Welcome, everyone, to Salina North. I am Mr. Victor, the assistant principal." To Katy's relief, the kids quieted down and listened while Mr. Victor went through a list of behavioral expectations. Dad had already read the rules to Katy from the handbook the secretary had given him and lectured her on the importance of following them. But she listened politely anyway.

When Mr. Victor finished explaining the school's rules, he said, "I know we have two transfers from Hutchinson, where they use a trimester system. Have any others transferred from a school with something other than the standard semester system?"

Katy raised her hand.

Mr. Victor smiled at her, his thick mustache hiding his upper lip. "What system did your school use?"

Katy blinked twice. "I—I'm not sure."

The man's smile broadened, making his mustache expand. "How many sections did you have?"

"Nine."

He reared back in surprise while the word *nine* was repeated around the room in disbelieving whispers. "You had *nine*?"

"Yes, sir." Pride squared her shoulders. Her school in Schellberg might have been small, but Gramma Ruthie and Dad had always emphasized how fortunate she'd been to have such a good teacher and a good school. "Miss Yoder taught all nine grades, and she divided us into— "

Raucous laughter covered the rest of her explanation. She looked around in confusion. What had she said that was so funny?

Mr. Victor clapped his hands again. "That's enough! Quiet down." He waited until the others quieted before turning back to Katy. "Did you have big tests right before winter break, and then again before school ended for the summer?" Something made his voice quaver, as if he was swallowing a laugh.

Katy hadn't realized a time of tests was called a "semester." Heat flooded her face. Her first day of high school, and she'd already encountered a new word: *semester*. She'd be sure to write it in her journal and remember it. "Y-yes, sir."

"Then your school operated on the standard two semester system." He lifted his gaze to include everyone in the room. "There has been some talk about our school integrating to a trimester system." Katy remained quiet while he explained the advantages and disadvantages of using three sections as opposed to two. Several students openly cheered when he mentioned that the trimester system made it possible for students to graduate early, but Katy wanted to cry out in protest. She'd just gotten here—she didn't want to be finished early!

"Now, let's discuss the bell schedules so you will know what to expect." Mr. Victor pulled three stiff posters from the corner and propped them on tall, silver easels. He held his hand toward the first poster. "Salina North operates on a modified block." Katy listened, her brow furrowed in concentration, as the man explained that the students would attend seven fifty-minutes-long sessions on Monday, but four ninety-minute sessions the remaining days of the week. She frowned at the posters. Something didn't make sense.

She thrust her hand in the air. "Sir?"

Mr. Victor looked at her. "Yes?"

"What is a block?"

A titter went around the table, and two boys elbowed each other, smirking. One boy said loudly, "A chunk of wood!" The titters turned to outright laughter. Katy wanted to glare at the boys the way she used to glare at Caleb Penner when he called her Katydid, but she kept her gaze aimed at Mr. Victor and waited for his answer.

Mr. Victor gave the boys a stern frown before turning to Katy. "We call the classes blocks. So, for instance, if you have English first hour, then English is block one for you. Does that make sense?"

Katy nodded. "Yes, sir. Thank you."

A slight smile curved his lips. He pointed to one of the posters. "Very good. Now— "

"Mr. Victor?" Katy waggled her fingers.

His hand remained suspended in front of the crisp white board. "Yes?"

"You said we all have seven blocks on Monday, but then on Tuesday and Thursday there's an eighth block. Why don't we have eight blocks on Monday?"

The man blew out a small breath and propped his hand on the edge of the poster. "Because not everyone has an eighth block."

Katy tipped her head.

"The eighth block is an ELO."

Katy wrinkled her brow.

"Extended Learning Opportunity. It's set up for students who need additional help in a subject."

"Oh! Tutoring." Katy nodded, relieved. "I understand. Thank you."

The man turned toward the chart and opened his mouth, but then glanced at Katy. "Any other questions?"

She shook her head, making her cap's ribbons dance beneath her chin. She caught the trailing ribbons and threw them over her shoulders.

"All right." He spent a little more time explaining the modified block system. "Since this is our first week and we only have two days, we're going to follow Monday's schedule today and tomorrow. That will give everyone a chance to become familiar with the campus and your teachers before starting fresh with the regular schedule on Monday. Now, please retrieve the printed schedule you were given at enrollment."

Katy unzipped her backpack and pulled out the pocket folder that held her schedule. Two students didn't have their schedules with them. She cringed, expecting Mr. Victor to berate them for being unprepared, but he simply instructed them to go to the office for duplicates. Katy watched the pair saunter out of the room, seemingly unconcerned about their missing schedules.

"Since you're new to our campus," Mr. Victor said, pulling Katy's attention back to him, "each of you will be matched with a returning student who will be your escort for the first week. He or she will offer assistance and answer questions."

Behind Katy, someone whispered, "I feel sorry for whoever gets stuck with the girl in the grandma dress." A girl giggled in response.

Katy pretended she hadn't heard, but her ears burned and she knew they were turning red. Caleb used to relish making her ears turn red. Hopefully the extended brim of her cap hid any changing color.

Mr. Victor strode to the door and opened it, then waved his hand. Several students filed into the room, and each of them held a small placard with a name on it. "Please introduce yourself to the person holding your name."

Katy leaned left and right, peering past shoulders until she found a placard with her name. She cradled her backpack and wove her way to a pleasant-looking girl with shoulder-length, rather messy blonde-streaked hair. "Hello." She pointed to the sign. "That's me."

"Hi, Kathleen." The girl smiled, flashing silver braces, and slipped the placard into the back pocket of her blue jeans. The movement pulled her striped shirt tight against her chest, emphasizing the curve of her bosom. Katy quickly averted her gaze. "I'm Shelby Nuss. I'll be showing you around." She gestured toward the door. "First hour has already started, but— "

Katy hugged her backpack tight. "We're *late*?" Miss Yoder had never tolerated tardiness. Would she have to take home a note on the first day of school?

Shelby grinned. "It's okay. The teachers expect the new students to show up late the first day because of orientation." She cocked her head toward the door. "Come on, though. The second block bell will ring soon, and you'll want to see where your first block class is located."

Katy avoided stepping on Shelby's heels as they headed down the hallway. Shelby glanced over her shoulder. She grinned again, and the overhead lights made her braces sparkle. "Come up here beside me. You don't have to stay back there." She caught Katy's elbow and pulled her forward. "Around here, if you don't push your way through, you might miss class. So don't be bashful, okay?"

Katy nodded, but inwardly she frowned. Pushing your way past people wasn't Christlike. Dad—and the deacons—wouldn't be pleased if she became self-serving. Her tennis shoes squeaked softly against the shiny tile floor as Shelby led her down a hallway lined with tall, narrow metal cubbies. At the top of each cubby's door, a small sign bore a stamped number. Shelby stopped when they reached 164B.

"All the sophomores have lockers in the B section. You should have a combination on your enrollment sheet to open the lock, but you'll probably only use the locker for your coat and ... um, necessities."

"Necessities?"

"You know—for that time of the month." Shelby's eyes skittered to the side and then back.

Katy's ears started burning again. Maybe she shouldn't ask so many questions.

"Most of us just carry our books in our backpacks because there isn't time to run to the lockers between every class." Shelby glanced at Katy's backpack, which was nestled against the modesty cape of her dress, and a small smile teased the corners of her lips. "Yours is real . . . nice, but you might want to get one with wheels. All the books can get pretty heavy."

Katy nodded, but she knew Dad wouldn't buy her another backpack. "Where's the first block class held?"

Shelby quirked her finger and led the way down a long hallway interrupted by doors with long, narrow windows. Katy couldn't resist peeking into classroom as they hurried down the hallway. They nearly reached the end before Shelby stopped in front of a door marked 173: BIOLOGY. Just as Shelby's hand closed over the door handle, the same clanging noise that had called everyone in from the front lawn blared again. It seemed to come from right above Katy's head.

She cringed, wishing she could drop her backpack and cover her ears. "What *is* that?"

Shelby gawked at her as if she'd suddenly sprouted green ears and a tail. "That's the *class bell*. That's how we know it's time to go to the *next class*."

"Bell?" Katy shook her head, her ears still ringing from the horrible attack of noise. "Bells go ring-a-ling. That thing goes *braaawnk!*" The classroom door flew open and students spilled into the hall just in time to hear the awful sound leave her throat. Laughter rang, even more offensive than the so-called bell.

Katy asked one more question. "Where is the ladies' room?"

Shelby pointed.

Katy turned and ran.

Chapter Three

The final bell of the day sent Salina High North's one thousand students spilling into the hallways in a mad rush for freedom. Katy crisscrossed her arms over her chest to avoid elbowing anyone and tried to worm her way to the edge of the hallway. If she tripped over a shoelace or one of the many rolling backpacks out in the middle of the sea of people, the crowd would trample her before they even knew she was down. Thank goodness for the comfortable sneakers on her feet!

Usually she bought her tennis shoes at Wal-Mart, but Gramma Ruthie and Grampa Ben had taken her to a shoe store in the big mall at Salina for her public high school shoes. The sales person called the blue and white leather sneakers "running shoes." Running shoes were *perfect* for this school!

Shelby trotted alongside Katy. Her shoulder bumped against Katy's, they were so close. "It can be pretty overwhelming at first, but you'll get used to it."

Katy forced a smile. "I suppose." What would Shelby think if she knew there were fewer people in the entire town of Schellberg than there were dashing through these hallways right now? Voices and the sound of shoes on the floor—squeaks from sneakers, clicks from heels, clomps from heavier soles—echoed from the walls and tile ceiling, creating a disharmonious racket. Katy couldn't wait to reach the yard and separate herself from the noise and confusion of the hallway.

Her backpack straps dug painfully into her shoulders. Each teacher had distributed a textbook and syllabus. Seven books created a lot of weight and strained the backpack to its limit. Katy hoped the seams didn't burst. But if they did, she'd be forced to buy a backpack with wheels, as Shelby had suggested. She'd find a black one.

When they reached the double doors leading to the outside, Katy charged directly to the center of the grassy yard and heaved a sigh of relief.

Shelby caught up to her and laughed. "Just think—one day down. Only one hundred and seventy-nine more to go."

Katy filled her cheeks with air and blew. She glanced at the milling crowd breaking into smaller groups to linger on the lawn or head toward the parking lot. Car doors and engines added a new harmony to the unique song of high school. "Thank you for helping me. I wouldn't have found my classes without you." Several times during the day Katy had offered a quick, silent prayer of thanks for Shelby's presence. "You've been very kind."

Shelby shrugged. "Just doin' my job as escort. No problem at all. I hope your stomach will be better tomorrow." She slipped her fingers into her pockets and glanced down the street. "You want me to stay with you until the bus gets here?"

Katy shook her head. "I'm fine. Thank you."

"Then I'll see you tomorrow. Bye, Kathleen." Shelby trotted off toward a cluster of girls, who huddled together to whisper and giggle. *Whisper and giggle about me?* Katy turned her back on the group, her ears burning. It was a wonder her ears hadn't burnt up, as many times as they'd been scorched today.

She slipped her backpack from her shoulders and leaned it against her legs while she waited for the bus. When it arrived, she clambered on board quickly. The driver was a man this time, with a square jaw and thick eyebrows. He didn't appear very friendly, so Katy didn't bother to introduce herself. The first seat behind the driver was open, and she dropped into it with a sigh.

The bus carried the same younger, noisy riders from the morning. The kids were even louder going home, and the driver yelled for them to settle down. His gruff order brought a momentary respite, but then gradually the voices rose again, earning a second reprimand. By the time the bus reached Katy's drop-off, her head ached from the bombardment of sounds.

Dad's blue pickup waited, and Katy nearly flew to the passenger side. She flung herself into the cab. "Hi, Dad!" Had she ever been so happy to see him?

"Hi, Katy-girl. How was the first day?"

"It was — " Her tongue froze. How *was* the first day? She'd been laughed at and stared at and stared past as if she were invisible. She'd thrown up her breakfast and been unable to swallow her lunch. She'd met teachers who seemed kind and others who seemed stern. She'd stepped into the world, and just like pond water on the first day of summer, it was *cold*. But past experience had taught her if she submerged herself in the water and moved around, her body adjusted. If she submerged herself in high school, she would adjust. She hoped.

"It was fine."

Dad nodded. He popped the gearshift into place and did a three-point turn-around to aim them toward their dairy farm. As they passed the schoolhouse, where two little boys bounced each other on the teeter-totter, Katy experienced a rush of loneliness. She gave her dad a pleading look. "Could I go visit Annika for a little bit?"

Dad rubbed his finger under his nose. "We have chores, Katy, and it'll be suppertime soon."

Katy bit her lip. Although Dad hadn't come right out and said it, she knew he had hoped to have her full-time help once she finished at the Schellberg school. Most families had several kids to help with chores — Dad only had her. He could have insisted she not go to high school, but he'd allowed her to pursue her dream despite his apprehensions. The least she could do was go straight home from school and help with chores before putting supper on the table.

"Okay." But frustration created an ugly knot in her empty stomach. Why couldn't Dad understand she needed to talk to someone about this day — to share the hurt of being laughed at, the confusion of the huge school campus, the strangeness of being surrounded by so many people, and the overwhelming eagerness to see what she could learn from the heavy books in her backpack?

When she was little she had followed Dad all over the place and talked to him about everything. But she wasn't little anymore, and it felt strange to share her innermost thoughts with him. If she couldn't go see Annika, she'd pour everything into her journal ... assuming Dad gave her time before bed. The older she got the more it seemed he only thought about the cows and what *they* needed.

Dad shot her a grin. "Gramma Ruthie brought over a special supper for your first day — chicken and stuffing casserole. You just have to heat it in the oven."

Ordinarily, Katy's mouth would water at the thought of digging into one of Gramma's delicious dishes. But for some reason her stomach rebelled. She covered her mouth with her hand and swallowed the uncomfortable feeling that rose from her belly. Tipping her face toward the open window, she willed the wind to chase away the nausea.

"Katy-girl?"

She glanced at Dad.

"You okay?"

"I feel kind of sick, Dad."

His face twisted into a worried scowl. Would he release her from evening chores? "Tomorrow you take your lunch box. It's probably the cafeteria food."

Katy almost laughed. Of course she'd still have to work. The cows had to be milked no matter how she felt. Besides, her own cooking was the culprit of her upset stomach — she hadn't eaten a bite of the cafeteria food. But she wouldn't walk into school with a lunch box. That would only give the kids another reason to point and snicker.

"The cafeteria food was fine. I was just too ... excited to eat, so my stomach is complaining."

"Well, let's get you home then and we'll have an early supper. The cows can wait a little bit to be put on the machines."

Warmth filled Katy's chest. Maybe Dad did think about her some too.

⁂

As Katy placed the last dripping plate in the dish drainer on the side of the sink, tapping sounded on the back door. She skipped through the narrow back foyer and spotted Annika on the little stoop outside the door. Katy let out a squeal of delight and threw the door wide. "Come in!" She grabbed Annika in a short hug and then pulled her into the kitchen.

Annika plucked an embroidered tea towel from the bar on the end of the counter and began drying a plate. "Mom said I could come see how your day at school went, but I had to make myself useful and not get in the way."

Katy grabbed the towel and plate from Annika's hands and pushed her onto a kitchen chair. "You don't have to dry my dishes. You probably already dried your family's dishes, didn't you?"

Annika nodded, the ribbons on her cap bouncing against her shoulders. "Yes. And we have a lot more dishes than you do!"

Katy imagined the pile of dirty dishes after a meal at Annika's house. Annika had five younger brothers and sisters, plus two older. The oldest was already married and living on his own farm, and her older sister's engagement had recently been published to the fellowship. She would marry in December, making Annika the oldest child at home. Annika often complained about how much her responsibilities would increase when Taryn left. "All the more reason why you shouldn't have to work over here too. Just talk to me while I get this finished up. What did you do today?"

Before Annika could answer, Dad clomped into the kitchen in his grimy choring coveralls. He glanced at Annika. "Oh, hello. You came to see Katy?"

Why else would she come? The question flitted through Katy's mind, but fortunately it didn't pass her lips. Dad never knew what to say to Annika, so he usually said something silly.

"Yes." Annika bounced up from the chair. "But I can leave if I'm in the way."

"No, no, sit down." Dad waved his hand at Annika. He tugged the coverall's zipper all the way to his chin. "I'm going to honk the horn to bring the cows in. Will you be out to help with the milking soon, Katy-girl?"

Katy pointed to the dishes in the drainer. "When I've finished the dishes."

"Hurry, hm?" Dad headed out the back door.

Annika watched him go. "It's too bad, isn't it, that your dad doesn't have any sons to help him."

Katy didn't answer. Gramma Ruthie had told her a long time ago it wasn't her fault that her mother had become dissatisfied with the Old Order life and left, but when people said things like Annika just had, she couldn't help but wonder if maybe her mom would have stuck around—or taken her with her when she left—if she had been a boy instead of a girl. "I suppose. But I can do almost anything a boy can." Defensiveness crept into Katy's tone. "I worked all summer beside Dad with the cows *and* did the housekeeping."

"Except you aren't here now to work with him. You're at school." Annika propped her chin in her hands, her eyes bright. "How was it? School, I mean. Was it fun?"

Katy wouldn't have called the day fun. She sought an appropriate response. "Intriguing. And enlightening."

Annika wrinkled her nose. "Why do you have to use such big words all the time?" Then she giggled. "Did you see any cute boys?"

Lately, Annika had started talking about Caleb Penner. All the time. Katy couldn't figure out what Annika saw in the gangly, big-eared boy. She thought about the boys who had imitated her "good morning" and laughed when she asked what a block was. They might have been cute from Annika's viewpoint, but they hadn't been cute to her. "Not really." She set a dry dish on its shelf and reached for a plate.

Annika's jaw dropped. "With all those kids? No cute boys?"

Katy shrugged, rubbing the towel across the plate's flowered face. "I didn't really look, Annika. You know what the deacons told me—keep myself separate." She sighed and her hands stilled on the plate. "It's going to be hard because there are *so many* kids. Walking in the hallway ... you can't even get through without bumping people. And they're so *loud*." She remembered the bell. For the first time she realized why the class-change buzzer was turned up so high—otherwise no one would hear it.

"But did you enjoy it at all?"

Katy closed her eyes, seeking an enjoyable moment. She looked at Annika and grinned. "Yes. When I got to put *my name* inside the cover of the textbooks. Kathleen Lambright. That means those books are *mine* for half the school year, maybe the whole year. And I can open them and read them and learn from them whenever I want to."

She danced toward Annika, swinging the tea towel. "And

the English teacher, Mr. Gorsky, said we'll be diagramming sentences. He showed us an example on the board, where a prepositional phrase became an adverb in the sentence, modifying the verb. And he didn't even mind when I asked him what it meant to modify a verb. He said— "

"You are so *weird*, Katy." Annika shook her head, her mouth pursed up like a prune. "All your learning ... What good will it do?" She held her hands outward, indicating the kitchen. "When you're finished over there, you'll come to a house like this one, marry a Mennonite man like your dad, and spend your days taking care of a family." She tipped her head to the side, crunching the ribbon against the shoulder of her green dress. "Is knowing how to ... to diagram a sentence with adverbs and prepositions going to make you a better wife and mother?"

Katy stared at Annika. Watching the teacher's hand form the lines of the diagram on the whiteboard in blue marker and then write the words in place had thrilled Katy. Words! And learning better ways to put them together! Wouldn't learning to diagram sentences make her a better writer? Why couldn't her best friend be excited with her instead of throwing cold water on her enthusiasm?

Swallowing her hurt, Katy formed a soft reply. "Learning more about the world and finding new ways to do things can only make me a better person. And that means I'll be a better wife and mother, don't you think?"

Annika sighed. "I wish you were here during the day, so we could see each other. Do you realize we've been together almost every day since we started school? Even in the summers we've gotten together. I missed you today."

Katy swallowed. She'd missed Annika too. She'd missed

having a friend to giggle with and eat with and *be* with. But then Annika's comment—*You are so weird, Katy*—repeated itself in her mind. Would it make any difference if she were here or at the public high school? Either place, someone thought she was an oddball.

"I better go help Dad with the milking."

"All right." Annika rose. "Maybe we can get together on Saturday? Walk down to the creek and catch crawdads?" She hunched her shoulders. "Caleb might be fishing ..."

Katy sighed. *Caleb again* ... "I'll probably have to help Aunt Rebecca in the quilt shop, but I'll ask."

"Oh, yeah, I heard she was mad about you going to school instead of working for her. She'd been counting on you."

Katy didn't need a reminder of Aunt Rebecca's disappointment. The woman had made her feelings quite clear. Katy followed Annika to the door. "Thanks for coming by." But was she really thankful? Annika's visit had only managed to stir up annoyance.

"Okay. See you later, Katy."

Katy watched Annika go, and that familiar sting attacked the back of her nose. She'd been so happy to find her friend on the little stoop, but now she was happy to see her leave. She pinched her nose, sending the sting away. She trudged to her bedroom to slip into her oldest dress, which she wore in the barn. Her gaze fell on the backpack resting against her desk. Learning was so important to her—important enough to petition the deacons for special permission to attend high school. But was it important enough to disappoint so many people? Dad needed her; Aunt Rebecca needed her; even Annika seemed to need her. Was she doing the right thing by going?

You are so weird, Katy. The sting in her nose returned, bringing with it the mist of tears. She pressed her fists into her eye sockets as she fought the urge to dissolve into frustrated wails. She didn't fit at the high school with her Mennonite dress and little white cap; she didn't fit in Schellberg because of her desire to learn. *God, is there anyplace I belong?*

Chapter Four

"There you go, Katy-girl. I'll see you around five."

Katy waved good-bye to Dad and then stepped from the dirt street onto the sidewalk that ran the length of Schellberg's limited business district. She stifled a yawn. Only a little after nine o'clock, and she'd already put in a good three hours of work between helping with the early morning milking, fixing breakfast and cleaning up, and doing two loads of laundry. When she finished working with Aunt Rebecca, she'd have to take the clothes from the line, iron everything, and get it put away before making supper. She sighed. Would she ever have time to herself?

Her journal had lain in her desk drawer, neglected, since the first day of school over a week ago. Her fingers itched to record her thoughts and feelings about the events of the past days, but responsibilities ate up every bit of time. *And complaining won't change it.* Setting her mouth into a determined line, she clumped to the door of Aunt Rebecca's shop.

The little bell hanging over the door tinkled a welcome when Katy entered the crafts and fabrics shop. The whir of Aunt Rebecca's sewing machine from its spot in front of the window abruptly stopped. Aunt Rebecca glanced at her watch and made a sour face. "The shop opened ten minutes ago, Katy. I expected you earlier."

Katy held her tongue. Aunt Rebecca was a complainer—nothing ever suited her. Telling her aunt she had other responsibilities would only lead to a lecture on honoring *every* commitment as doing it unto the Lord. Katy had listened to many similar lectures in the past, the most recent one last Saturday when she'd dared to mention she needed to leave early so she could write a "My Favorite Summer Memory" essay for her English class before preparing Dad's supper. She had no desire to be scolded again. It was better just to apologize and move on.

"I'm sorry, Aunt Rebecca."

Her words didn't hold much remorse, but Aunt Rebecca nodded and flapped her hand toward the curtained doorway at the back of the neatly arranged shop. "Well, you might as well get started. I have a stack of fabric bolts on the work table in the back. Cut the first ten yards of each bolt into fat quarters and package them."

Katy didn't need further direction. She'd been helping in Aunt Rebecca's shop since she turned thirteen—the age deemed old enough to handle responsibility. She pushed the yellow gingham curtain aside and entered the organized workspace. Once behind the curtain—and out from under Aunt Rebecca's watchful gaze—she allowed herself a rare moment of pouting.

She whisked the length of pink calico across the work table and reached for a yardstick and scissors while inwardly grumbling. Just how many responsibilities did one girl need? The day after her thirteenth birthday, Gramma Ruthie had stopped sewing Katy's dresses. She'd also ended her daily trek to the farm to prepare meals, do laundry, and clean.

All Dad had to do was see to the cows.

All Aunt Rebecca had to do was run her shop — her oldest two girls, fourteen-year-old twins Lola and Lori, did the housekeeping.

But Katy ran a household, sewed her own clothes, helped with milking, helped her aunt, *and* did homework! Surely less was expected of every other girl in the community.

Snip, snip, snip ... She trimmed away eighteen inches from the bolt, cut the long strip crosswise into two halves, then set the pieces aside. She measured the next length, her mind drifting to the stack of homework awaiting her: Twenty algebraic equations to solve, a dozen compound sentences to diagram, a short report on China's exportation to the United States to research and write, the parts of a maple leaf to label ...

"Katy!"

Katy dropped the scissors onto the wooden tabletop and clapped her hands to her beating heart. "Aunt Rebecca, you scared me."

"I meant to." Her aunt scowled from the doorway. "You've been standing there for a full minute, staring into space and doing nothing."

How do you know? Were you wasting time standing there watching me? Katy bit the end of her tongue to hold the words inside.

Aunt Rebecca pointed to the work table. "That fabric won't cut itself."

"Sorry," Katy mumbled, picking up the scissors again. "I was — "

"Daydreaming, I know." Aunt Rebecca tsk-tsked and plunked her fist on her hip. "Katy, the Fall Festival is September nineteenth, only three weeks away. My preselected fabric packs are always the best seller. I need at least three hundred of them ready to go." She pursed her lips, making the lines around her mouth look like the ravines Katy had studied in geography last year.

Aunt Rebecca's scolding voice continued. "If you worked here every day, you might have time to daydream, but since you can only come on Saturdays, there isn't a minute to waste. Get busy!" She dropped the curtain back in place. Moments later, the sewing machine took up its whir again.

Katy's shoulders sagged. Another reminder of how much she was needed during the week. Her hands remained busy at the monotonous task while her mind played over the past seven school days. Although she'd become familiar with the large campus—she could find her way to every class on time—she still felt like a ... well, a Mennonite in a room full of non-Mennonites. *Or*, her thoughts sniped as she considered the behavior of some of the students, *a Mennonite in a room full of heathens.*

Then she scolded herself. *Be nice, Katy. They aren't all heathens*. She'd learned Shelby's father was a minister. Of a Baptist church, but a minister anyway. And a group of students, led by a girl named Jordyn and a boy named Nick, met every Wednesday morning in the home economics classroom for a Bible study. Shelby had invited Katy to join them, but since she rode the bus, she couldn't make it in time.

The overt staring had come to an end for the most part

at least, which was a relief. Katy had never cared much for people gawking at her—it always made her ears hot. But the opposite of gawking was ignoring, and she suffered a great deal of *that*. Her hands slowed in stacking the cut pieces of calico. What made her invisible to people outside of Schellberg? Was it her white mesh cap and homemade caped dress, or something deeper? Something beneath the surface that screamed *weird*?

Suddenly a memory flashed through her mind. She'd been very young. Maybe four. Tall enough to reach a cup and the water spigot if she used her little red stool, but not yet school age. She remembered creeping downstairs after bedtime to get a drink of water, and mumbled voices from the front room pulled her in that direction. Although she knew children weren't supposed to intrude on adults' conversations, she couldn't stop herself from hiding behind the doorframe and listening. Her little-girl heart had nearly broken at Dad's anguished tone as he talked to Gramma Ruthie.

"When will they stop it, Mom? They either stare at me or act like I'm not there. They make me feel like an outsider in my own community."

Gramma Ruthie's soothing voice had responded as tenderly as if she were talking to little Katy. "They don't know what to say to you, Son. They feel sorry and confused, so they look past you to avoid their own feelings. It will stop when the newness wears off."

Katy had tiptoed away, wondering who had made her dad feel so terrible. Not until years later did she understand he was complaining about the community's response to her mother's abandonment. Gramma Ruthie had been right — over time, people stopped whispering. Then Katy gave a jolt. People had stopped until she asked permission to attend high school. She'd started the whispers again.

Someone pulled the curtain aside, and Katy quickly snatched up the pile of neatly cut fabric pieces. "I'm sorry, Aunt Rebecca. I was just getting ready to — "

But instead of Aunt Rebecca's disapproving face peering through the doorway, Gramma Ruthie's bright eyes sparkled at Katy. "Well, Katy-girl, I see you've got quite a stack cut. Would you like me to help you fold and package them?"

Katy didn't need help — she knew how to fold the quarters into neat squares and layer them to show a thumbnail view of each fabric. But Gramma Ruthie would visit with her while they worked, making the time fly. "Yes, please!"

The pair settled on tall stools on opposite sides of the worktable and began sorting the fabric pieces into pleasing combinations. "So ... tell me about school."

Katy grinned. Gramma Ruthie was old — almost seventy — but sometimes she acted like a young girl. Of all the people in Schellberg, excluding Dad of course, Katy loved Gramma Ruthie the most. If she couldn't have a mother, at least she had her gramma. But then her smile faded.

"Gramma, am I hurting Dad by going to school?"

"Hurting your dad? Why do you ask that?" Gramma's wrinkled hands paused and she gave Katy her full attention.

"I'm afraid — " Katy glanced toward the curtained doorway. Would Aunt Rebecca listen and criticize? She dropped her voice to a whisper. "I know he works hard and could use my help. And I know he worries I'm going to get pulled away, like my mom was. Should I just stay home and not go to school?"

Katy's chest ached as she waited for Gramma Ruthie's reply. She respected her grandmother so much — if Gramma said Katy should stay home, she would do it, even if it meant her heart would ache for the rest of her life.

"Tsk, Katy ..." Only Gramma Ruthie could *tsk* without making it sound like she was scolding. "Yes, your dad could use your help. But he could also hire help. What's important is God's will for you — school, or working with your dad." She pointed her arthritic-bent finger at Katy. "In all of your life, Katy-girl, there will be doors opening. Some doors are happenstance — just a chance opportunity that flies in without notice — and other doors are God-doors. You have to learn to recognize the difference and walk through the God-doors. Because if we resist a God-door, we lose out on His blessing."

"But how can you know which is which?" Katy had been so certain going to school was a God-door. The deacons had talked for two weeks before giving her permission. No one else in her community had ever asked to go beyond ninth grade. Surely the idea had been God whispering to her heart rather than happenstance. But since she'd walked through the door, things had become complicated.

"You'll know the same way you know anything ... from the peace in your heart." Gramma slid a stack of folded squares into a plastic bag and stapled it shut. "You know Proverbs sixteen verse seven. 'When a man's ways please the Lord, he — ' "

"'... maketh even his enemies to be at peace with him.'" Katy finished the Scripture with a sigh. "I know the verse, Gramma Ruthie, but does that mean if some people aren't at peace, then the person hasn't followed the Lord's ways?" She could count at least a half dozen people who weren't at peace with her attending school ... including herself.

For a moment Gramma Ruthie peered directly into Katy's eyes, her face pinched into a thoughtful frown. Finally she blew out a little breath and waved her hand. "You ask hard questions, Katy." She chuckled. "But then, you always have. That's what makes me think this idea of going to school is right for you—I've never seen a more inquisitive mind."

Inquisitive ... Katy liked the sound of that word better than the one Aunt Rebecca had used in the past: snoopy.

"As long as you can add knowledge to your head without affecting what's in your heart—without losing your faith—I don't see anything wrong with what you're doing. But it isn't for me to say. You are going to have to pray hard and figure it out for yourself."

Katy groaned. "Why can't it be easy?"

Gramma Ruthie laughed, shaking her head. Her black ribbons swayed beneath her softly sagging chin. "Ah, Katy-girl, anything worth having isn't easy. Would you like one more piece of advice from a busybody old lady?"

Katy grinned. Gramma Ruthie wasn't a busybody. She leaned forward eagerly.

"Words from God Himself: 'Thou wilt keep him in perfect peace, whose mind is stayed on thee.'" Gramma Ruthie gave a solemn nod. "You think first about pleasing

God, Katy-girl, and everything else will fall into place ... for you, and for your dad. Now," she said as she reached for another square of fabric, "let's get these bags stuffed so we can walk next door and get a sandwich from the café. We *might* even bring one back for Rebecca!"

Chapter Five

Katy waved to the little kids as the big yellow bus pulled away from the high school. Their cheerful farewells rang in her head, making her smile. The bus ride had been much more pleasant since she'd befriended the younger students. She'd used a simple ploy — bringing along a loop of yarn and twisting it through her fingers to create Jacob's ladder. The trick had intrigued the kids on the bus, just like it had done with her little cousins.

When she'd pulled out a variety of loops from her backpack and showed the kids how to make their own Jacob's ladders, she'd instantly won their attention and affection. Only the junior high–age boys rebuffed her, but she didn't mind. They sat way in the back and left the others alone.

She headed toward the main building, skirting groups of loitering students. No one even glanced her way as she passed the clusters of laughing, jabbering kids. She stifled a sigh. If only she could win the affection of her peers as easily as the little kids on the bus. But a Jacob's ladder made of string wouldn't impress high school kids.

Since students weren't supposed to enter the building before the opening bell, Katy leaned against one of the tall windows that flanked the double doors and gazed across the yard at the others. At the Schellberg school, all of the kids from littlest to biggest mingled as a single group. It was almost like a family gathering every day.

But at Salina High North, distinct groups formed. After two weeks of attending school, Katy could easily identify many of them: the athletes — or "the jocks," the debate squad, the popular crowd, the partiers, and the nerds. At lunch the second day of school, a girl named Jewel had suggested Katy go sit with the nerds. "You'd fit right in with your weird fashion style," she'd said. Shelby had immediately hushed her, which made Katy feel a little better, but the comment still stung. Although the word "nerd" had been a new one, Katy knew Jewel hadn't meant it as a compliment.

"Hi, Kathleen." Shelby bounded across the concrete courtyard, a big smile on her face. Shelby was always smiling even though sometimes her upper lip got caught in her braces. She'd just laugh and unhook it, then smash a ball of wax onto the wires to keep it from happening again. "You found the best place to stand — out of the sun. Mind if I join you?"

"No." Katy scooted her backpack closer to her legs to give Shelby more room. She hadn't expected the girl to continue talking to her after the first two days, when she'd been assigned to escort Katy around the school. But to Katy's delight, Shelby continued to seek her out. Someone at this school realized she was real.

Shelby parked her wheeled backpack next to Katy's. "Did you get all of those sentences finished for English?"

Katy asked. Shelby shook her head, the shorter layers of streaky blonde hair dancing around her cheeks. "I *hate* all this diagramming. I'll be glad when we move past it."

Katy decided it might be best to keep her enjoyment in diagramming secret. No sense in making herself even more of a nerd. "I finished my homework early so I could work on a new dress." Aunt Rebecca had let her choose fabric as payment for her long hours of packaging fabric kits. She'd chosen a deep lilac with tiny white and yellow flowers.

Shelby's gaze flicked from Katy's caped bodice to the hem of her skirt that ended two inches below her knees. "You make your own clothes?"

Katy nodded, uncertain by Shelby's tone whether she was impressed or amused.

"Wow, that's pretty cool." Shelby flashed another silver smile. "I made a pillowcase one time, but it came out all crooked. I never used it." She laughed. "I could never make a whole dress."

"I could show you." Now where had *that* offer come from?

Shelby laughed again. "Thanks, Kathleen, but I better pass. I'd probably mess up your machine big time." She propped her shoulder against the window. "Can I ask you a question?"

Katy gave a slow shrug. "Sure."

"Do you only have one pattern? I've noticed all your dresses are the same, except for the colors. I'm not trying to be rude—I'm just curious." She glanced again at Katy's dress. "Is there, like, some rule in your church that you have to use this pattern?"

"I don't know that it's a rule ..." Katy bit on her lower lip for a moment, forming her answer. "This style is modest. It conceals a woman's ..." Unconsciously, her gaze whisked to Shelby's chest and up again. Her ears went hot. "Her ..."

"Attributes?" Shelby contributed with a grin.

Katy sagged with relief. "Yes. *That.*" She looked across the grounds at the variety of skin-tight tops, low-cut blouses, and printed phrases that enticed one's eyes to a girl's attributes. She turned back to Shelby and finished seriously, "We try not to encourage men to look lustfully at us, which would be causing them to sin."

Shelby nodded thoughtfully. "Makes sense." She shifted to plant her back on the large window pane. "I gotta tell you, Kathleen, I kind of envy you. On being able to sew, I mean. My mom has this quilt hanging in the family room. Her grandmother made it. Even when I was a little kid, I'd stand and stare at all the squares and triangles that form the pattern and wish I could make something like that." A tinkling laugh spilled from Shelby's lips. "But after the whole pillowcase fiasco, there's no way I'd try to sew a quilt."

"You could start with a small one." Katy thought about the kits in Aunt Rebecca's shop. "Maybe a little nine-patch wall hanging. It's all straight seams, so it would be a good starting project."

Shelby waved her hand, as if shooing away Katy's suggestion. "Thanks but no thanks. I think I'll leave the sewing to you." She tipped her head. "Did you have home ec at your old school?"

"Home ec?" Katy crunched her face.

"Yeah, home economics — like, learning to cook and sew and all that stuff to keep a house running."

"Oh!" Katy laughed. "No, in Schellberg, you learn home ec at *home,* from your parents."

"So your mom taught you to sew?"

Katy's ears heated up. She licked her lips. "No. She's dead." She hadn't lied—her mother *was* dead, killed in a car accident four years after leaving her and Dad. But she wouldn't explain all that to Shelby.

Shelby straightened from the window, her eyes wide. "Oh, Kathleen, I'm sorry. I didn't know." She touched Katy's arm. "That must be rough."

Katy hadn't expected such kindness. No one in Schellberg ever acknowledged Katy's loss. If her mother's name was mentioned, it was always a sad or disapproving comment about her decision to run away. She swallowed. "Sometimes. But I have my gramma, and she's a great seamstress. She taught me to sew. She could teach you too."

Shelby released a soft snort. "I don't know about that ..."

Something drifted through Katy's mind, and before she could stop it, the thought tumbled out. "On September nineteen, our town is having the annual Fall Festival. Gramma Ruthie will be at my aunt's fabric store, demonstrating quilting techniques for visitors. Maybe you could come and watch, and my gramma could help you pick out an easy quilt kit to get started. The festival's a lot of fun. Corn shucking, carriage rides, homemade apple cider and root beer ..." Even worse words followed, encouraged—no doubt—by Shelby's sincere sympathy. "If you wanted, you could spend Friday night at my house and go with my dad and me on Saturday."

Now she'd done it! She bit down on the end of her tongue to keep anything else from flying out of her mouth. What would Dad say when he found out she'd invited a girl from high school to spend the night? She'd often had Annika over, but Annika was Mennonite. Shelby was Baptist. If Dad had a hard time talking to Annika, he'd be stricken mute in Shelby's presence! She decided to retract the invitation quick before she got herself in trouble.

"Shelby, I— "

The opening bell blared, covering Katy's words. Shelby pulled up the handle on her backpack and gestured Katy toward the doors. They trotted to keep ahead of the throng pressing behind them. Shelby hung onto Katy's elbow. "Thanks for inviting me to the festival, Kathleen. I've seen it advertised in the paper, but I've never gone. I'll check with my parents tonight and see what they think. Can I answer you tomorrow?"

Katy nodded and walked into class. She slipped onto her tall stool in the biology lab, her pulse racing faster than a horse galloping across the pasture in early spring. What had she done? She knew she was supposed to ask permission to have guests. And she'd not only given an invitation without asking first, she'd invited someone from outside of her fellowship to stay at her house! She'd have to find a good way to confess to Dad what she'd done.

Her hands shook as she removed her biology book from her backpack. The teacher began his instruction, but Katy couldn't concentrate. Maybe Baptists didn't let their kids go to a Mennonite's farm. Maybe Shelby's parents would say no. Hope whispered around the edges of her heart. Her pulse slowed a bit.

No sense in talking to Dad unless Shelby said yes. She'd just wait until tomorrow.

"Kathleen, can we join you?"

Katy looked up from her lunch. Shelby and three of her friends—Cora, Trisha, and Bridget—stood at the end of the table with lunch trays in their hands. Shelby hadn't been in any of their morning classes, and Katy had wondered if she was sick. Although she was glad Shelby was all right, her heart started to pound as she remembered yesterday's impulsive invitation. It might be best to avoid Shelby until she forgot Katy had asked her to spend the night. But several chairs separated Katy from those eating at the other end of the long table. She'd look like a snob if she told the girls no. Plus, having Shelby and her friends around would distract her from Jewel, who had been making fun of Katy since she sat down.

Forcing a nod, she said, "Sure."

Shelby took the seat next to Katy and the others lined up across from her. "See anything different?" She offered a huge smile.

Katy gaped. "I can see your teeth! The braces are gone!"

Cora snickered and nudged Bridget. Bridget rolled her eyes. Katy's ears started to heat.

Shelby smiled even bigger, putting her open hands on either side of her cheeks to turn her face into a sunshine. "Yeah, got them off this morning. It feels really weird too, after wearing them for four years." She ran her tongue over her teeth and then laughed. "That's why I wasn't here." She opened her milk carton. "I'm glad to have them gone, but my teeth are kinda sore from being poked on. I don't think I can bite into those chicken nuggets."

"I'll take 'em," Cora said.

Katy opened her mouth to remind Cora that the school rules said no food sharing, but Cora reached across and scooped Shelby's chicken nuggets into her hand. One bounced off the tray and onto the table, sending a shower of crisp crumbs in Trisha's direction. Cora giggled. "Oops!"

"Stop making a mess, Cora." Trisha brushed the crumbs toward Cora. Several flew into her lap.

"Don't!" Cora squealed, rearing back. Her shoulder slammed into Bridget, who was lifting her milk carton for a sip. Milk sloshed down the front of her shirt.

"Cora!" Bridget slammed the carton onto her tray and reached for her napkin.

The lunch monitor strode by their table and sent a warning glance their way. The three hunched their shoulders and giggled. Their behavior reminded Katy of how she and Annika used to play around during lunch break, and a smile twitched on her lips.

Shelby nudged Katy with her elbow. "Hey, Kathleen, I talked to my parents about that ... what did you call it? Fall Festival?"

Katy's smile disappeared. She nodded.

"They said it would be fine for me to go."

Suddenly the trio across the table became very interested in Shelby and Katy's conversation. Cora said, "Go where, Shelb?"

Shelby continued as if Cora hadn't spoken. "You usually ride the bus, right? I can't ride the bus—district policy—but my dad said he'd drive me out to your place if you give me directions. Or ..." Her eyes widened, and her smile grew. "Hey! You could get permission from your dad to skip the bus, and you could ride with me to your place. Then you could just show my dad where you live."

Bridget tapped Shelby's arm. "What're you talking about?"

"Never mind." Shelby brushed Bridget's hand away. "What do you think, Kathleen?"

Katy stared, slack jawed, at Shelby. *I think I'm in really big trouble.*

Chapter Six

Katy waited until Dad finished his second serving of cherry crisp before approaching the subject of Shelby spending the night. Fixing his favorite dessert was a deceptive tactic, and guilt made her hands tremble as she reached for his scraped-clean bowl and his spoon, but she needed him to be in an especially good mood.

"Dad, you know the Fall Festival is coming up ..."

Dad sipped his coffee, his eyes half-closed. "Mm-hm?"

Katy busily stacked the dirty dishes next to the sink, maintaining a casual tone. "And I was thinking that maybe it would be nice to invite a girl from the high school to go to it with me. Her name is Shelby Nuss." She glanced over her shoulder. Dad's eyebrows lowered. She hurried on. "She's interested in learning to quilt, and I think Gramma Ruthie could help her."

"A girl from the high school? She's your friend?"

Katy considered Dad's question. Was Shelby her friend? Shelby was kind to her. She sat with Katy in class and in the cafeteria, and walked with her in the halls sometimes. She was the closest thing to a friend that Katy had at her school. She swallowed. "Yes. I suppose she is." *Or could be . . . maybe.*

"Then I should get to know her."

Katy knew that meant Dad wanted to be sure he approved of Shelby, but she didn't mind. Not if it meant she wouldn't have to take back her invitation and embarrass herself. "Can she come here on the Friday before the festival and stay all night?"

Now Dad's eyebrows shot up. "All night?"

"And Annika too. She hasn't stayed over since early in the summer." Although Katy hadn't originally intended to have both girls, the idea made sense. If Annika were left out, she'd be jealous. It would be better to include her. Inviting Annika would also prove to Dad she wasn't trying to leave her Mennonite friends behind.

"*Two* girls?" Dad made a face and put his coffee cup down. "I don't know."

"I'll still help with milking and all my other chores." Annika and Shelby could entertain each other while she helped Dad. She clasped her hands beneath her chin. "Please? We'll be so quiet, you won't even know we're here."

Dad's lips twitched. "Katy-girl, you aren't *that* quiet by yourself."

Katy grinned. Dad didn't often joke with her, so it meant he wasn't upset about her request. "So they can come? Shelby *and* Annika?"

He pressed his palms to the table, pushing himself from the chair. "I suppose it will be all right."

Katy sucked in a happy breath.

"We need to arrange for me to meet this girl's parents before the nineteenth."

She blew out the air, her shoulders sagging. "How can you do that? She lives in Salina. And you have to milk in the evening ... Can't you just meet her dad when he drops her off here?"

Dad gave Katy a puzzled look. "Her parents would bring her without meeting me beforehand?"

Katy paused. Since Shelby's parents had already given permission for her to spend the night with Katy, they obviously hadn't felt the need to meet Katy's dad ahead of time. "Well ... I guess they would ..."

Dad shook his head. "That isn't wise. A parent shouldn't send his child to a stranger's house." His thick brows formed a V on his forehead. "No. I can't have a girl stay here without first meeting her parents." He handed Katy his empty coffee mug. "Does her family have a telephone?"

Katy had seen a little pink cell phone in Shelby's backpack. If she had a cell phone, then her parents certainly had a telephone at their house too. "Yes."

"Get their number for me, and I'll call her dad from the grocery store and arrange a time for us to meet."

"But, Dad— "

"You can't have her here until her parents and I have met, Katy, and that's final."

Katy watched Dad round the table and head out the back door. She bit her lower lip, worry making her stomach churn. When Dad talked to Mr. Nuss, would he discover Katy had invited Shelby before asking permission? If so, she'd be in trouble with Dad. And with Shelby. She walked to the sink and gave the water spigots a vicious twist.

I might as well forget about having Shelby over now. Even

if Dad doesn't make me uninvite her, Shelby won't want to come after Dad calls her parents. No other dads have to meet her parents ahead of time. Now she'll think I'm weird, just like Jewel and all the other kids at that school do.

Even though Katy was supposed to wash the dishes and then help with the evening milking, she shut off the water, left the dishes in the sink, and ran to her room. She'd gone too long without spilling her feelings into her journal. One word — one ugly word — seemed to chase her up the stairs: *Weird ... weird ... weird ...*

Katy stood behind Dad and chewed her thumbnail while he reached across Mr. Nuss's desk to shake hands. Her ears still burned from the embarrassment of finding Dad parked in the bus loading zone at the close of the school today. A couple of the jocks had made fun of their pickup and of Dad's suit and black, flat-brimmed hat.

Why had he worn his Sunday suit to meet Shelby's parents? He wouldn't have stuck out so badly in his work trousers, plaid shirt, and billed ball cap. Her heart turned over. He'd dressed up out of respect and to make a good impression on the Nusses. She should be grateful, but humiliation washed the gratitude away.

Shelby's father ran his hand down his striped tie and pointed to two matching chairs that sat side-by-side against the wall. "Please sit down, Mr. Lambright and Kathleen." He settled himself in the squeaky black chair behind the desk and linked his fingers over his stomach. His brown eyes matched Shelby's, as did his smile. If Katy hadn't been so nervous, she would have smiled back when he winked at her. "Thank you for meeting me here at the church. It would probably be more comfortable at the parsonage, but my secretary is under the weather and wasn't able to come in today. If I left the office, there wouldn't be anyone to man the phone. We don't want to miss any calls in case someone needs assistance."

Katy began nibbling her pinky nail. Mr. Nuss's constant talking was pointing out how very different the Baptists were from the Old Order Mennonites. The Mennonite meetinghouse didn't have a pastor's study, as Shelby had called her dad's office. No secretary answered telephone calls at their meetinghouse — there wasn't even a telephone in the building. And Katy had no idea what Mr. Nuss meant by "parsonage." Maybe she should start carrying a dictionary in her pocket.

"Shelby is excited about the festival," Mr. Nuss continued in a cheery voice. "We saw it advertised in the newspaper last year, shortly after we moved here, and we discussed going then. It looks interesting, but the janitor reminded me that Saturday is a preparation day for Sunday." He laughed softly. "My wife is the janitor here at the church, and she isn't shy about enlisting the help of her family to get the building spotless for Sunday morning services."

Dad held his hat in his lap and gave a solemn nod. "It's good to take proper care of the Lord's house. When it's our turn to clean the meetinghouse in Schellberg, we do our best work too." He glanced around the shelf-lined walls. From floor to ceiling, books filled the dark-stained shelves. The sight made Katy's chest expand with envy. What must it be like to own so many books? "You are an ordained minister, Reverend Nuss?"

"That's right, through the Southern Baptist Convention—but please call me Brother Tim. And your first name is ...?"

"Samuel," Dad provided.

"Samuel," Mr. Nuss repeated. "Well, it's good to have this chance to get acquainted. Shelby has told us a lot about your Kathleen. She's hoping Kathleen can join the Christian Students' Club. I'm sure she's told Kathleen about it already."

Dad flicked a quick, questioning look at Katy. Katy inserted, "It meets before school on Wednesdays. Since I ride the bus, I can't get there in time."

"Oh." Mr. Nuss puckered his lips. "That's too bad. Well, maybe next year, if you drive yourself to school ..."

Katy almost giggled. Dad owned one vehicle—their old blue pickup. He hadn't let her learn to drive yet. She supposed she could saddle her personal means of transportation, her ten-year-old mare, Shadow. But even if Dad allowed her to, she wouldn't ride Shadow to school. The kids would laugh her out of the parking lot.

Dad tapped his hat on his knee. "Rev—Brother Tim, I wanted to meet you and talk some before we have your daughter stay at our house. Katy—"

Katy cleared her throat.

Dad frowned. "*Kathleen* wants to be friends with Shelby. I must be sure it won't be harmful to her before I give my approval."

Katy held her breath. Would Mr. Nuss be offended?

Shelby's father leaned forward and propped his elbows on the desk. His chair creaked in complaint at the sudden movement. "Do you mean you want to be sure Shelby won't try to convince Kathleen to do something that would be against your beliefs?"

Dad nodded. "Staying true to our teachings is very important. Kathleen spends time at school with children who have been raised very differently. This will certainly have an effect on her. But if she forms close friendships, there is greater opportunity for her to adopt other habits and behaviors, some of which may not be appropriate."

Katy gnawed in earnest on her left thumbnail. She'd already nibbled the right one clear to the quick.

Dad went on, "I don't want to tell the girls they can't be friends. Friends are important. I just need to be sure Shelby understands that Katy ... er, Kathleen ... is Mennonite, and she will stay Mennonite."

Mr. Nuss's face didn't lose its friendly expression. "Samuel, I appreciate your honesty. Your desire for Kathleen to maintain her Mennonite beliefs mimics my desire for Shelby to hold fast to her Christian standards. She's been taught since she was very young that she needs to honor God with her words, actions, and attitude. If at any time you feel she is behaving in a way that would be harmful to your daughter, I would want you to tell me right away. My responsibility as Shelby's father and her minister is to keep her on a godly path."

Dad didn't smile, but Katy sensed him relaxing a bit. He said, "I also want to make certain that you have no concerns about Shelby spending time with my daughter and me. There is no ..." Dad lowered his head for a moment. "No wife in my home."

Katy flicked a glance at Reverend Nuss. The brief flash of sympathy in his eyes reminded her of Shelby's reaction when she'd said her mother was dead. The Nusses might not be Mennonite, but Katy liked them. They were nice people.

Dad met the reverend's gaze again. "Kathleen and I have been alone for several years. If the situation makes you uncomfortable—having your daughter staying in a home with only a father and daughter—then we'll understand that you'd rather not have Shelby spend the night."

"Shelby told us Kathleen's mother had passed away." Mr. Nuss sent a quick, understanding smile in Katy's direction. "I'm sorry for your loss. Shelby has other friends who, for various reasons, live with a single parent. We've told her if she's in a situation that makes her feel uncomfortable that she can call at any time and we'll come and pick her up. Does that sound reasonable to you?"

"I think that makes good sense," Dad said.

Mr. Nuss leaned back in his chair and placed his hand over the telephone receiver on the corner of his desk. "Are there any specific rules your family follows that Shelby needs to hear before she comes to your house? I can call her over right now and we'll discuss them together."

Dad put his hand on Katy's arm. "My daughter knows the expectations, and she can share these with Shelby. Do you have rules that should be enforced while your daughter is with us? I want to show consideration for your beliefs as well."

Mr. Nuss smiled. "Thank you, Samuel. I appreciate that. Our family strives to obey the commandments written in God's Word. Honoring her parents extends to honoring other adults in authority." For the first time, his face turned stern. "If she behaves inappropriately, please let me know. There will be consequences here at home."

Katy listened in amazement. Mr. Nuss just said, nearly word for word, what her dad had told Miss Yoder every day on the first day of each school year at the Schellberg school. He'd told the principal at Salina High North the same thing when he enrolled her at the high school.

While she watched Dad and Reverend Nuss shake hands in parting, a realization crept through her brain. The two might be dressed differently and attend different places of worship, but in some ways they were very much alike.

Dad turned in at the Gehrings' farm on the way home from meeting with Shelby's father so Katy could invite Annika to stay over the night before the festival. The Gehrings' property bordered the Lambright dairy farm, and although their houses were a mile apart, the girls were accustomed to walking to visit one another. Still reeling from the amicable meeting between Dad and Mr. Nuss, Katy couldn't wait to tell Annika how well it had gone. She bounced out before the pickup had rolled to a complete stop.

"Don't stay long, Katy," Dad admonished, leaning out the truck window. "You have chores waiting. Get permission from Annika's mom and then walk straight home."

"Yes, Dad. Thanks!" Katy skipped up the dirt pathway that led to the farmhouse and hopped up on the unrailed porch. Annika's house and Katy's were both two-story farmhouses built in the early 1920s, but Annika's looked older with its peeling paint and porch that slanted toward the south. Katy had written a poem about Annika's tired-looking house — exhausted from its door being opened and closed all day long by the many occupants. Miss Yoder had given Katy high marks on the poem, but Annika hadn't like it much.

Just before she knocked on the wood-framed screen door, one of Annika's brothers came around the corner of the house. "Hi, Katy. Annika's in the barn. We got a new batch of kittens, and the mama finally brought them out of hiding." He grinned, showing two missing teeth. "They're cute. Go see 'em."

Katy had seen plenty of barn kittens, but it never grew old. They were always so sweet when they were little. She dashed to the barn and found Annika kneeling in a corner stall. Two kittens stood in her lap, batting at the strings of her cap. She looked up and grinned when Katy approached.

"Hi! There are two more over there, if you want to play with them." She pointed to twin orange and white balls of fur coiled against their mother's stomach, fast asleep.

Katy sank down next to Annika but didn't disturb the kittens. If she started playing, she'd forget to hurry home. "I came to see if you wanted to spend the night next Saturday."

Annika's face lit up. "Really? Then we could go to the festival together. That would be fun. I'll go ask Mom." She pried the kittens' little claws loose from her apron and plunked them next to the mama cat.

Katy followed her toward the house. "I hope you can come. It will be kind of a party since a girl from Salina High North is coming too."

Annika froze in her tracks. "Oh?"

Despite the sun beating down, Katy experienced a chill.

"Yes. Her name is Shelby Nuss, and Dad just talked with her father. Mr. Nuss gave Shelby permission to spend the night. I thought it would be fun for all of us to get to know each other."

Annika folded her arms over her chest. "Why?"

"Because ... Because ..." Katy licked her dry lips and held her hands outward. "Why not?"

"I don't know this girl. I don't go to high school. Why would I want to spend time with her? It'll be weird, staying the night with *her* there."

There was that word again. Katy huffed. "Annika, you're my best friend. I want you to meet the girl who's been nice to me at school. She wants to come so she can learn about quilting. If she learns, we could have fun making things together — maybe form our own little quilting bee."

Annika rolled her eyes, reminding Katy of Jewel at the high school. Katy marveled that Jewel's eyes were still in her head, she rolled them so frequently. She turned to walk away. "But if you don't want to come ..."

Annika grabbed Katy's arm. "Oh, don't run off. I'll ask." She scuffed her way toward the house, her head low. "At least it'll get me away from my pesty brothers for a little while ..."

Katy waited on the porch while Annika went in to get permission. The joy of seeing her father and Mr. Nuss shake hands and agree to let her and Shelby be friends melted away. Why couldn't she hold on to peace for more than a few minutes at a time?

Chapter Seven

"Well ..." Katy wiped her mouth with her napkin and dropped it on her plate. Plastering on a bright smile, she looked from Annika to Shelby. "Dad will need my help with the milking soon. Do you two want to stay here in the kitchen or come out in the yard?" Earlier, Dad had prayed for the meal, then filled a plate and taken it to the barn, claiming the need to do some work out there. But Katy knew he felt funny sitting at the table with her guests. She added, "It's probably cooler outside than it is in here since I heated things up with the stove."

Katy had deliberately fixed tuna-noodle casserole with buttered bread crumbs on top for supper. Annika loved egg noodles with tuna, canned cream of mushroom soup, and frozen peas stirred in. Preparing Dad's favorite dessert had worked well to put in him the mood for company, so she'd employed the same technique to win Annika's approval. But it hadn't worked so well. Although Annika had eaten three hearty servings of the casserole, she'd barely mumbled two words since she arrived. Her sober face was starting to rub Katy the wrong way.

Shelby dropped her napkin on the table and bounced

to her feet. "I'd love to go out and see the cows. I've never lived on a farm, so this is all new." She turned to Annika, who remained glued to her chair. "Are—are you going out to see the cows, Annika?"

Katy couldn't decide whether Shelby sounded hopeful because she wanted Annika to agree or because she wanted Annika to refuse.

Annika pushed a leftover pea back and forth on her plate. "I've seen cows before. You two go ahead."

"Are you sure?" Katy asked. She wanted to make sure Annika understood she wasn't being left out.

Shelby looped her hair behind her ears, revealing a little gold hoop high in the cartilage of her right ear. "Why don't you come outside, Annika. Kathleen's right—it is pretty hot in here." She tugged the hem of her bold turquoise shirt and flapped the fabric.

Annika glanced up and then back at her plate. "No, thank you," she replied stiffly. "You two go ahead. I can do the dishes for you or maybe find a book and read."

"Okay then. C'mon, Shelby." Katy propelled Shelby toward the back door and sent a murderous glare over her shoulder at Annika. Out in the yard away from Annika's listening ears, Katy sighed. "I'm sorry Annika's being so rude. I think she's jealous."

"Ya *think*?" Shelby laughed.

"If she's really making you uncomfortable, maybe I should ask her to go home ..."

Shelby shook her head and slipped her arm through Katy's. "No, don't do that. It'll just cause problems for you later on." She frowned toward the house. "She really needs to chill, but don't worry about it. I'm infringing on her territory. Once she figures out I'm not trying to steal you away, she'll get over it and be okay."

Katy wasn't so sure about that, but she was glad Shelby wasn't offended. They moved to the fence and rested their arms on the top rail. Inside the fence, the black-and-white cows munched stubs of grass and nosed each other, waiting for the horn to signal milking time. One cow lifted her head and pinned her gaze on Shelby. The big animal stopped mid-chew, grass hanging from one side of her mouth, and stared, unblinking.

Shelby pointed to the cow. "Is she looking at me?"

Katy nodded. The cow, rapt in examining Shelby, didn't shift a muscle.

Shelby released a nervous giggle. "Why is she looking at me like that?" She ran her hand over her face. "Do I have a noodle stuck on my chin or something?"

Katy grinned. "You're fine. It's just that cows are very curious."

Two more cows lifted their heads and looked toward the girls. They, too, keyed in on Shelby. Now three cows gave her their unwavering attention.

Shelby shifted under their intense scrutiny. She dropped her voice to a whisper. "The way they're staring at me is totally bizarre."

"Not really. They know you're new around here so they're checking you out."

Shelby flicked a glance at Katy, and her expression turned apologetic. "I'm starting to understand how you must have felt that first day, with everyone staring at you like you were some alien from Mars." She touched Katy's arm. "I felt so sorry for you."

Katy didn't answer. Had Shelby befriended her only out of sympathy? That didn't seem like a very good basis for a friendship.

Suddenly the truck horn blared—one long blast. In unison, the cows lifted their heads and turned toward the sound. Then they started trotting around the barn, forming a single-file line.

Shelby stared in amazement. "Look at them! Lining up like first graders heading to recess. How do they know to do that?"

Katy shrugged. "They just do." She grabbed Shelby's elbow. "I have to go help Dad, but you can watch from the tank room. C'mon." She deposited Shelby in the room that housed the large, refrigerated milk tank. A square plate-glass window gave a view of the milking station with its four milking machines clustered in the center of the concrete floor.

After tugging a pair of men's coveralls over her dress, since she hadn't had time to change, she joined Dad. He took one side of the station, and she the other. The cows shuffled through the wide opening at the far side of the milking room and crossed the floor in pairs. Without prompting, they each positioned themselves next to one of the electric milking machines.

Working as adeptly as Dad on the opposite side of the room, Katy attached the suction cups to the cow's udders and flipped the switch. Milk flowed from the tubes into a large glass orb above the machine, then through clear tubes overhead into the large holding tank in the milk room.

Shelby stood with her face pressed to the window, her eyes wide. As the cows were released, they passed the observation window on the way to the corral. Each one paused and gave Shelby a curious look before clopping outside. Shelby smiled and waved at them as they ambled past the window. An hour and a half later, when the last cow had been milked and released, Shelby met Katy and Dad in the barn.

"That was totally awesome!" Shelby dashed to the barn's opening and looked out at the cows, which now mingled in the fenced corral beside the barn with Katy's horse, their udders slack beneath their bellies. "I had no idea you could *train* cows. But here they came, all lined up and ready to go." She spun around, flashing an astonished grin to both Katy and her dad. She gestured wildly while she spoke. "And they just stepped up to the machine, right where you needed them, and then took themselves outside when they were done." She shook her head. "Amazing!"

Dad chuckled, rubbing his finger beneath his nose. "Oh, not so amazing. When their sacs are full, they're uncomfortable. They know the machine will ease their discomfort. They also know they'll get fed right afterward. They're just earning their supper."

"So that milk ..." Shelby waved her hand toward the milk room. "Where does it go from there? Do you bottle it yourselves?"

Dad's lips twitched. "Oh, no, we don't bottle it ... except for what we use. A truck comes every other day and takes it to a processing plant where it's homogenized and bottled. Our work ends with convincing the cows to give us their milk." Katy's eyebrows flew upward in surprise. Had Dad just had a conversation with Shelby?

Dad turned to Katy. "I'll get them fed—you spend time with your guests now, Katy-girl." He strode past Shelby and left the barn.

Shelby grinned, tipping her head. *"Katy-girl?"*

Katy's ears heated. "Yes. That's his nickname for me." She paused a moment, then began a hesitant explanation. "See, my mom was Kathleen too, and she went by Kate most of the time, but Dad called her Katy. When I was born, Dad started calling me Katy *girl* to keep me separate from my mom. And it just kind of ... stuck."

Shelby giggled. "I think it's cute. Way more cool than what my dad calls me for a nickname."

"What?"

"Promise you won't tell?"

Katy traced an X on her chest with her finger.

"Puddin'-pot."

Katy burst out laughing. "Why Puddin'-pot?"

"Because I was so fat when I was little, my tummy was as wobbly as a pot of pudding." Shelby cupped her stomach with her palms and pretended to joggle it. The girls shared a laugh.

Katy shook her head, looking Shelby up and down. "You aren't fat now." Shelby's cap-sleeved shirt and capri-length jeans, while not as tight-fitting as those worn by some other girls at school, did nothing to hide Shelby's slender figure.

Teasingly, Shelby struck a pose with one hand on her hip and the other behind her head. "Why, thank you." Then she laughed and clapped her hands once. "Well, it was fun to watch the milking. What else is there to see?"

"We can take a walk around the farm, if you want to.

We have a pond about a mile behind the house, and there are some old stone buildings that are fun to explore." Katy peeled off her coveralls and hung them on a hook. "We can go everywhere except the bull's pen. He doesn't care for visitors."

"Great! Let's go!" Shelby grabbed Katy's arm and charged out of the barn. Then she came to a halt. "Oh, we should get Annika, shouldn't we?"

Katy's heart warmed toward this Baptist girl — the visitor trying to make the host feel at home. "You stay here. I'll go get her." If Annika made a fuss, she wanted to protect Shelby from witnessing it.

She trotted to the house and found Annika standing at the kitchen window, looking out. "Shelby and I are going to take a walk down to the pond. Come join us."

Annika stuck her nose in the air. "As if she'd want to see the pond." She folded her arms over her chest. "Besides, I thought that was *our* spot. That's what you've always called it — *our* private getaway spot."

"Well, then, we won't go to the pond. We'll just walk the fence line and talk."

"About what? If you two talk about school, I won't know what you're talking about; if we talk about things in Schellberg, *she* won't know what *we're* talking about." Annika huffed. "This is stupid, Katy, trying to make us get along. We don't even know each other!"

"And you won't get to know each other unless you try." Irritation sharpened Katy's tone. "She's willing — why can't you be?"

Annika stomped her foot, and tears glittered in her eyes. "She goes to a school with ... how many people,

Katy? Over two hundred just in your class. There are all kinds of girls she can be friends with. But all *I* have is you. We're the only two girls our age in all of Schellberg. If you and she become friends and start spending time together, then—" Annika looked toward the door.

Katy looked too. Shelby stood on the stoop, peeking through the screen. By the sheepish look on her face, Katy knew she'd heard Annika's outburst. Katy's ears burned hotter than the casserole dish in the oven. What should she do? Before she could think of anything, Shelby squeaked the door open and stepped into the kitchen.

"Hey. I wasn't trying to eavesdrop—honest. It's just that the breeze has picked up a little, and I wanted to get my jacket before we explore." Her gaze flitted back and forth between Katy and Annika. "But ... can I just say something here?" She didn't wait for an answer. "Annika, I'm not trying to steal Kathleen away from you. You guys have been friends since ... forever, and I totally respect that. But don't you think Kathleen could benefit from a friend or two at the high school? I mean, it's not much fun to be completely alone."

Shelby turned to Katy. "And, Kathleen, if my being here is a problem, I can call my dad." She patted her pocket, where her cell phone created a bulge. "He'll come get me, no questions asked. I'd really like to go to the festival tomorrow and meet your grandma and everything, but ..."

Shelby looked at Katy. Katy looked at Annika. Annika stared at the floor. No one said anything. Suddenly the screen door slammed and Dad clumped into the kitchen. He came to a stop when he spotted the girls standing in a silent circle.

"What's going on?"

"Nothing." Katy answered quickly. "We were just trying to decide what to do next—go to the pond ..." She gave Annika a challenging look. "Or walk out to the old rock buildings and look around."

"Oh." Dad popped his hat off his head, ran his hand over his hair, then plunked the hat back in place with the billed brim low over his eyes. "Well, whatever you do, don't forget you'll want to turn in early so you're well-rested for tomorrow's festival." He headed around the corner, and in seconds they heard his feet on the stairs.

Katy crossed her arms and looked at Annika. "Well? What are we going to do?"

Annika shrugged, running her finger along the edge of the sink. "I don't care."

"To be honest, I'm having fun and I *don't* want to go home." Shelby's bright tone contrasted Katy's and Annika's subdued voices. "How far is it to the stone buildings?"

"About half a mile." Katy glanced at Shelby's thick-soled flip-flops. They were cute, but they wouldn't work well for hiking. "You'll need sneakers, though. We'll be walking through some tall grass. You can borrow an old pair of mine."

Shelby shot Annika a wobbly smile. "Is that okay with you then, Annika? To explore the old buildings?"

Annika didn't meet Shelby's gaze. "Sure. Whatever *you* want is fine ..."

"Great!" Shelby sat at the kitchen table and kicked off her flip-flops. "Go get those tennis shoes, Kathleen, and some socks too!"

Annika sniffed.

Katy rolled her eyes and headed for the stairs. Was Shelby unaware of Annika's sarcasm, or was she simply choosing to ignore it? Either way, the minute she could get Annika alone, that girl was going to get a piece of her mind, long-standing friendship or not!

Chapter Eight

It was a disaster — a total disaster — from the very start! Katy slashed the words into her journal. A flashlight propped on its side illuminated the page with a triangle of white light. Across the landing, Dad slept, unaware of Katy's nocturnal activity. Katy knew she should be sleeping too — they had service in the morning, and yawning in the middle of the sermon would earn her a stern talking-to. But she couldn't shut down her thoughts.

She glanced at her bed, envisioning Annika and Shelby last night lying with their backs to one another. There'd been enough space between them for Katy to crawl in if she'd had a mind to. Her anger returned again as she remembered Shelby's futile efforts to bring Annika out of her doldrums. Eventually Shelby had quit trying and ignored Annika, which put Katy in the middle — a very uncomfortable spot. And the tension had carried over from Friday night to Saturday.

Turning back to her journal, she recorded every humiliating second of the festival. Annika giggling and flirting with Caleb Penner but ignoring Shelby; Aunt Rebecca berating her — in front of Shelby! — about spending the day "playing" instead of helping with customers in her shop; Dad making her and Shelby come home before they had a chance to take a carriage ride because the cows needed milking ... Just once, couldn't the cows wait?

She ended the lengthy paragraph with *Was it too much to expect a pleasant day with my two best friends?*

Her hand stilled as she stared at the words *two best friends*. Could a person have *two* best friends? And was it even fair to give Shelby such an important title when they'd only known each other a few weeks?

Staring across the deeply shadowed room, Katy envisioned Annika in her white mesh cap and dangling ribbons next to Shelby with her shoulder-length, flippy hair. Two girls, so different. But not once during her stay had Shelby balked at following Katy's routine of chores or Bible-reading with Dad at the end of the day. When Dad had prayed before sending the girls upstairs to bed, Shelby had bowed her head reverently, as if she'd prayed with Dad dozens of times. Even though her clothes were different, Shelby's behavior had fit.

Katy snorted. If Annika visited Salina High North, she'd stand back with her arms folded over her chest, just like she did when they went shopping at Wal-Mart. Annika didn't like mixing with the world. And apparently she didn't like "the world" mixing with her.

With a disgruntled huff, Katy slammed the journal closed and flipped the little switch on the flashlight, plunging the room into darkness. She felt her way to her bed and climbed in, then lay wide-eyed, staring at the ceiling. Two friends from two worlds. But from now on, she'd have to keep them separate. It was like oil and water. They just didn't mix.

Katy awakened the next morning to a loud banging on her door. Her heart in her throat, she jumped out of bed. Dizziness attacked at the sudden movement, and she stumbled to the door and opened it. Dad stood on the landing in his Sunday suit, his scowl directed at Katy.

"What are you doing? You aren't even dressed. I milked without you because I thought you were inside fixing breakfast. We'll need to leave for service soon."

She groaned. How could she have slept so late? She never slept late on Sunday. "I'll be down to fix your breakfast in a minute!" Katy slammed the door and scurried to dress. Her hands shook as she brushed her hair into a bun and pinned a cap in place. Dad would be plenty upset with her ... and rightfully so. She knew better than to be so irresponsible.

When she ran downstairs, she found Dad at the table eating a bowl of cereal. She retrieved her own bowl and spoon and poured corn flakes. She prayed and then ate under Dad's disapproving silence. He remained silent all the way to church, and he sent her to her bench without his customary smile.

Katy sat amongst the women, her back straight, with her Bible open in her lap. On the other side of the church, Dad sat with the men. She sensed his irritation with her from across the aisle, and she had a hard time concentrating on the singing and sermon. At the close of the service, she knelt to pray with the others, and she asked God's forgiveness for her lazy behavior this morning. She vowed never again to shirk her duties.

Out in the yard, she ambled up beside Annika, who stood talking with Katy's twin cousins. As soon as she joined them, Annika spun on her. "Lori and Lola agree with me. You shouldn't have brought that girl to stay the night."

Katy bit down on the end of her tongue. Of course Lori and Lola would side with Annika. Although they were Katy's only girl cousins near her age, she'd never been particularly close to them. Because they had each other, they didn't seem to need anyone else.

Forcing a calm tone, Katy said, "*That girl*'s name is Shelby, and she came for the festival just like hundreds of other people come each year. She had a right to be here."

"The others don't come because you invited them," Lola said.

"And the others didn't stay overnight in your house," Lori added. She leaned close, her green eyes snapping. "Mom says you're looking for trouble, Katy, spending so much time with worldly girls. She's watching you to make sure you don't pick up bad habits."

Katy wanted to tell her cousins that Shelby was kinder and easier to get along with than Aunt Rebecca. What would they say if she told them that by attacking her they weren't following the Bible teachings of avoiding conflict? She imagined their surprised faces if she managed to speak the words aloud, and a giggle escaped.

"It isn't funny, Katy!" Lola crossed her arms and glared at Katy. "Romans twelve, verse two says, 'And be not conformed to this world.' "

" '... But be ye transformed by the renewing of your mind, that ye may prove what is that good, and acceptable, and perfect, will of God,' " Katy finished automatically.

Then she tipped her head. "Maybe it would be good for you"—she glanced across all three scowling faces—"and Aunt Rebecca to remember your behavior is supposed to be acceptable to God. Would He approve of you rejecting Shelby just because she isn't of Mennonite faith?"

Lori gasped. "In Ezra, the Israelites were told to separate themselves from the foreign people around them. We're not supposed to mix, Katy!"

"Why do you suppose we form our own communities, away from worldly people?" Lola stared at Katy, wide-eyed. "So that we can keep ourselves separate and follow our faith without distractions."

Katy resisted rolling her eyes. She was older than the twins; she didn't need them explaining the Mennonite ways to her.

"Lola's right," Annika chimed in, her arms folded so tight against her stomach that her skirt poofed out below her arms. "In the gospel of John, Jesus tells His followers they are not of the world."

Katy blew out a frustrated breath. "And in Mark, the disciples are instructed to go into all the world *and* preach the gospel. How can you do that if you never enter the world?" Several people turned to look the girls' direction, and Katy realized she was raising her voice. She swallowed more angry words before they could leave her lips.

Annika tossed her ribbons over her shoulders and looked down her nose at Katy. "But you aren't a disciple, and you aren't preaching the gospel at that school. You're just a foolish girl getting pulled in by worldly ways. And you'll be sorry, Katy!" The trio whirled and stormed away, leaving Katy alone.

Annika's words haunted Katy the remainder of the day and continued to play around the fringes of her mind on Monday as she left the bus and walked through the groups of students. She leaned against the door, waiting for the bell, while troubling thoughts plagued her.

As much as she didn't want to consider any truth in her friend's exclamation, she couldn't help but wonder if she was displeasing God by walking among the worldly. And since she was here, shouldn't she be sharing Him with those she encountered rather than living her faith quietly? Deep in thought, she didn't notice anyone approach, and she jumped when someone touched her arm.

Shelby grinned. "Hi! I didn't mean to scare you. You were miles away." Her forehead puckered. "Are you okay? You look kind of ... I don't know ... really sad."

"I'm just tired." Katy hadn't lied. She'd fallen asleep very late on Saturday, and she had gotten little sleep Sunday night. She straightened and faced Shelby. "Shelby, I want to apologize for— "

Shelby held up her hand. "Don't even start. You didn't do anything wrong, so you don't have reason to apologize." She laughed softly. "One thing my dad preaches *a lot* is that we can't control what someone else does—we can only control ourselves. Annika is who she is. You can't change it, and you're not responsible for her actions."

Katy nodded slowly. She'd have to give Shelby's words some thought.

Shelby went on, "Besides, I came over to say thanks for letting me stay at your house. I really did have a good time in spite of Annika. I hope sometime you'll let me come back, because I'd like to ride your horse." Another laugh trickled out. "And I'd like to, you know, return the favor."

Katy gave Shelby a bewildered look. "Return the favor? What does that mean?"

"I'm having a slumber party next Friday night — the whole gang, kind of as a way of welcoming Jewel into the family."

Now Katy shook her head. "Jewel? You mean — " She clamped her jaw closed. She wouldn't say something unkind, and she couldn't think of anything kind to say about Jewel. The girl had a way of looking at Katy, with her lips curled into a little snarl and her eyes squinty, that made Katy want to crawl under a desk and hide.

"Yep, Jewel." Shelby's expression turned serious. "She's staying with us as a foster child. My parents have always done foster parenting, but Jewel's the first one we've taken in since Dad and Mom got certified for Saline County. She's not real thrilled about being placed with a preacher's family, but when you're a foster kid, you don't have any choice. You go where they put you."

Katy knew about fostering. A single lady from Schellberg kept children whose parents couldn't care for them. But she only took babies and little kids, not teenagers. "But why is she with you? Isn't she big enough to take care of herself?"

Shelby made a face. "I'm not allowed to say much — it's supposed to stay private. But just let me say that Jewel's home life is pretty bad. Her mom has all these boyfriends coming and going, and things go on that could be, well, dangerous for Jewel. She needs a safe place to stay. So she's with us."

Katy's heart twisted in sympathy for Jewel. She didn't want anything bad to happen to the girl. But she couldn't imagine sharing her home with someone like her. Jewel was so ... *hard*.

"But anyway," Shelby continued, "Mom and Dad said it would be good to have some kids over and include Jewel so she feels like part of the family. So ... can you come to my slumber party? If you do, it'll be me, you, Bridget, Cora, Trisha, and Jewel. We'll make popcorn and drink pop and stay up all night. It'll be fun."

Katy held her breath for a moment. Oh, how she wanted to go! But Annika's comments about being separate and Dad's irritation with her for oversleeping on Sunday jumbled up to create a huge roadblock in her mind. "I don't know if I can. I—I'll have to ask Dad."

Shelby grinned. "That's fine. Ask him tonight and let me know tomorrow. That'll give you time to notify the bus driver that you won't be riding Friday afternoon—you can just come home with me after school. My dad said he'd run you back to Schellberg Saturday afternoon when we finally wake up." She grinned. "Trisha is staying the whole weekend, but I know you'd rather go home and go to your own church."

Katy's heart warmed at Shelby's understanding. She thought about the sour looks on Annika, Lola, and Lori's faces yesterday. Sadly, she realized she felt more comfortable with Shelby—a worldly girl—than with her cousins and lifelong friend. Shouldn't it be the opposite?

"Let me know, okay?" Shelby grazed Katy's shoulder with her hand. "I'm gonna go walk in with Jewel. See you in class, Kathleen."

Chapter Nine

"Grampa Ben!" Katy quickly waved good-bye to the bus kids and then skipped to her grandfather's truck. She curled her hands over the driver's side windowsill. "Why are you picking me up?" Joy at seeing her grandfather melted as a fear attacked. Her heart skipped a beat. "Did something happen to Dad?"

Mindful of Sunday morning's mishaps and Dad's aggravation with her, Katy had climbed on the bus that morning without wishing her father a good day. If she'd wasted her last chance to give him a kind word, she'd never forgive herself. Her heart pounded while she waited for her grandfather's answer.

"No, no, he just got hung up at the Feed and Seed, waiting for Mr. Bornholdt to finish tallying his bill. So he asked if I'd come get you. He didn't want you standing alongside the highway."

Katy nearly collapsed with relief.

"But there you are, standing alongside the highway anyhow." Grampa Ben grinned, his faded gray eyes crinkling. "So step off the road an' get in the truck, Katy-girl."

With a giggle, Katy ran around the hood and climbed

in. Grampa Ben's truck was even older than Dad's, and the gears ground out a complaint when he put it into drive. The truck bucked twice, like a horse trying to dislodge its rider, and then smoothed out as they headed toward Katy's home.

"Well, Katy-girl ..." Grampa hollered over the truck's engine noise. "Is that school goin' good for you? Learnin' what you want to?"

Katy could have said she was learning things she hadn't expected, but she didn't want to explain her meaning. "Yes, sir." She told him about her favorite class — English, where they examined the purpose of each part of speech and ways to put words together for maximum impact. "Our teacher says we'll be reading novels and dissecting them the second nine weeks — examining characters and plot and motivation — and then we'll start writing our own stories. I'm excited about it!"

Grampa chuckled. "Ah, Katy-girl, you and your words ..."

Katy held her breath, wondering if Grampa would call her weird. But instead he asked about her other classes, and time slipped by quickly. They pulled onto Katy's lane, and Dad's pickup sat in front of the barn. Katy waited until Grampa coasted to a stop, then she leaned across the seat and gave his soft cheek a quick peck. "Thanks for the ride, Grampa! I'll see you in service Sunday."

"Sure thing, Katy-girl. Bye, now."

Katy ran to the house and left her backpack right inside the back door, then darted out to the barn. Dad was busy heaving bales of hay into a stack along the north wall. She paused for a moment, watching him and marveling. Dad was getting old. He'd celebrated his forty-seventh birthday over the summer, just three days after her sixteenth. But he still worked as hard as men half his age.

Love for Dad welled up inside of her, and before she could stop herself she ran across the barn and threw her arms around his middle, pressing her cheek against his firm back.

His movements stilled, his arms held outward from his body. After a moment, he gently tugged loose of her grip and turned to face her. Puzzlement showed on his face. "Katy? You okay?"

She laughed. Apparently it had been far too long since she'd hugged him if he thought there was something wrong. "I'm okay. I just wanted ..." She hung her head and played with one ribbon. "I'm sorry I didn't tell you good-bye this morning. And I'm sorry about yesterday. I won't sleep through my chores on Sunday again. I know it made the morning stressful for you." She stared at his feet and waited for a lecture on responsibility.

He put his hands on his hips and looked toward the barn doors instead of at her. Finally he sighed. "A person's entitled to a late morning of sleep now and then. You work hard, and I suppose you earned those extra hours of rest."

She peeked at him. He wasn't smiling, but he wasn't frowning either. "So you forgive me?"

"I forgive you. And I'm sorry if I was cross with you. Sometimes I worry ..." His voice drifted off for a moment, his brows low. He finished, "Sometimes I worry that I expect too much from you between taking care of the house and working with the cows. And now with you in school, and needing study time ..."

Guilt pricked again. "Dad, I— "

He removed his hat and bounced it against his trouser

leg. "There's gonna be some changes around here, Katy-girl. I talked to Mort Penner, and he said his boy Caleb could use some extra money. So he'll be driving out twice a day to help with the milking. That way you don't have to worry about it. You'll still have to do the housekeeping, but you'll have more time for your studies."

Katy held her breath. Caleb Penner at her house twice a day?

"Come summer," Dad went on, "we'll go back to you helping. But for now, having Caleb here ought to make things a little easier for you."

Katy thought about Annika's infatuation with Caleb. She wasn't sure that having Caleb here would improve things in her rocky friendship with Annika. But she nodded. "Thanks, Dad. It'll be nice not to have to worry about the cows."

"But you still have to worry about supper." Dad's lips twitched into a sideways grin that made him look years younger. "So head into the house and get started. I brought home a fresh chicken from the market. I was thinking we could have fried chicken and mashed potatoes with gravy."

"Yes, sir!"

The rumble of an engine reached their ears, and Dad moved to the barn opening. Katy followed and peeked out. Caleb Penner's black sedan pulled onto the property. Dad glanced at his wristwatch and gave a satisfied nod. "Five o'clock, just as his dad promised." He strode forward to meet Caleb.

"I'm going on in to start supper, Dad." Katy ignored Caleb's freckled grin and scurried into the house. She was already on shaky ground with Annika over her friendship with Shelby; she wouldn't add being friendly with Caleb to Annika's list of grievances.

Dad closed his Bible and bowed his head. Katy followed suit. She listened to him offer his evening prayer, thanking God for the day of honest toil and asking for protection through the night. For as far back as she could remember, her day had ended just this way—listening to Dad pray. Security and peace wrapped around her, as warm and cozy as a quilt on a winter night.

"Amen," Dad said solemnly, then looked at her with a tired smile. She knew what he'd say even before his lips formed the words. "Good-night now, Katy-girl. Sweet dreams." He rose.

Katy bounced up and held out her hand. "Dad, before you go up to bed, can I ask you about something?"

"What's that?" He covered a yawn with his hand.

"Shelby Nuss asked if I could spend the night at her house this coming Friday ... kind of a turnabout-is-fair-play invitation. I'd go home with her after school, and then her dad would bring me back Saturday afternoon." Katy raised her shoulders and held them there, waiting for Dad's response.

Dad crunched his face into a thoughtful scowl. "Saturday afternoon? But what will Aunt Rebecca do if you aren't there to help her on Saturday?"

Katy slowly lowered her shoulders. "Um, there's probably not much to do since the festival was last week. Just clean-up stuff. Maybe I could work through the evening—Mr. Nuss could drop me off at Aunt Rebecca's shop when he brings me to Schellberg. And then I could just stay in town with Gramma Ruthie and Grampa Ben and go to church with them in the morning. That way you wouldn't have to come get me."

The plan made perfect sense to her, but Dad frowned. "I know I said you wouldn't have to do milking anymore, but that doesn't mean you don't have other responsibilities here."

"I know, Dad." Katy nibbled her lower lip while he worked his jaw back and forth in silence.

Finally Dad sighed. "You talk to your aunt, and if she says she doesn't need you all day on Saturday, then you can go."

Katy sucked in a happy breath.

"But," Dad added, his voice stern, "staying in Salina with Shelby doesn't mean you can do all of the things Shelby can do. Even at Shelby's house, you follow our rules."

"Yes, Dad!"

Dad headed upstairs to bed. Katy zipped around the house and turned out all the lights then went to her room. She slid into her desk chair and pulled out her journal and a pencil. *If Aunt Rebecca says no, it will be very hard not to be disrespectful. Even though Jewel will be there too, I really want to see what worldly girls do at a sleepover …*

Chapter Ten

Aunt Rebecca had said yes. Katy unzipped her backpack and removed her clean dress, socks, and underwear. The clothes were wrinkled from spending the day crowded next to her books, but there'd been no other way to transport her items from home to Shelby's. She shook out her dress, crunching her lips into a scowl. Aunt Rebecca would certainly complain if she showed up at the shop looking rumpled.

She turned to Shelby, who was unrolling fat sleeping bags across the basement's carpeted floor. "Do you have an iron and ironing board I could use in the morning?"

Jewel lounged on the lumpy sofa that stretched along the back wall of what Shelby called a "rec room." She rolled her eyes. "Ironing? Nobody irons anymore."

Somebody must, because I do. Katy held the comment inside and focused on Shelby.

"Sure." Shelby beckoned Katy with her finger to follow her. "Our laundry room's back here." Katy trailed Shelby down a short hallway to a small room that smelled clean and soapy. A cute wallpaper border of a clothesline strung with tiny shirts, aprons, and pants lined the walls right below the ceiling line. Katy eyed the automatic washer and dryer that sat side by side beneath a shelf and battled a wave of jealousy. Wouldn't she love to use something like that in place of the old wringer washer in her farm's washhouse?

Shelby opened a narrow door and pointed to an ironing board that hung on the wall. "It just folds down, and the iron is over there." She pointed to the shelf above the washer. "Feel free to use it whenever you want to." Then she lowered her voice to a whisper. "And don't tell Jewel, but Mom irons everything—sheets, shirts ... even Dad's handkerchiefs for Sunday." She winked.

Katy giggled and followed Shelby back to the rec room. Jewel's eyes were closed, but she held her arms stiffly across her chest, feigning sleep.

"Cora, Trisha, and Bridget will be here between five thirty and six, as soon as Cora's mom gets off work and can pick them all up," Shelby said as she tossed bed pillows on top of the sleeping bags. The floor turned into a giant, puffy patchwork quilt. "Mom's planning on ordering pizzas, so I hope that's okay with you."

"I love pizza." Katy sat in an overstuffed chair and crossed her ankles. "Aunt Rebecca makes the best cheese and mushroom pizza. Whenever we have a family birthday party, she always brings it, and she says the birthday person gets the first slice." She giggled. "Usually that ends up being his *only* slice, because people snatch it right up."

"Why don't you buy pizza instead of making it?" The lazy question came from Jewel, who didn't bother to sit up or open her eyes.

Katy glanced at her. "Because there isn't any place to buy pizza in Schellberg. You either make it or go without."

Jewel snorted. "I'd just go without. Or buy frozen."

Katy made a face. "Frozen pizza? I bet it tastes like cardboard."

"Better than having to *make* it." Jewel yawned and rolled to her side, pointing her backside at Katy.

Shelby caught Katy's eye and made a funny face. Katy covered her mouth to keep from laughing out loud. Jewel was annoying, there was no doubt about that, but if Shelby could laugh about it, so could she.

When Shelby finished arranging the sleeping bags to her satisfaction, she and Katy played a board game. The Nusses had a large selection of games on a shelf in the corner of the basement room, many of which Katy had played before. But Katy chose one she'd never seen because of its funny name. Jewel gave up on pretending to sleep when Katy and Shelby got too noisy in rolling dice, giggling, and sending the other one's game piece back to its home base.

A little before six, footsteps pounded on the basement stairs, alerting them to the arrival of Cora, Trisha, and Bridget. A round of squeals erupted when they burst into the room. Shelby and the three newcomers linked elbows and bounced in a circle on top of the sleeping bags, giggling like a bunch of ten-year-olds.

Katy sat in the chair and watched them. How would it feel to grab hold and bounce with them? She glanced at Jewel, who also observed the noisy quartet. Even though Jewel's eyes were narrowed and her lips set in a familiar sneer, Katy believed that Jewel also wanted to be a part of the circle.

Shelby dropped to the floor, pulling the others with her. She panted and laughed at the same time. "Okay, now that we're all here, let's plan our evening."

Cora unzipped a brown and pink polka-dotted duffle bag. "I brought the longest, most romantic movies from my mom's collection."

Jewel sat up and plucked one of the slim cases from Cora's hands. "Oh, yeah, I saw this in the theater when it came out. It's good. Let's watch it first."

Shelby took the case from Jewel and pulled her lips to the side. "Sorry, gang. No movies this time." She flicked a glance at Katy. "Kathleen's not allowed to watch TV."

Jewel gawked at Katy. "Are you kidding?"

All five girls looked at Katy. Her ears began to burn. She uncrossed her ankles and crossed them the opposite way. "In our fellowship, we don't watch television."

"But why?" Jewel sounded horrified.

Katy shrugged. "It's ... not appropriate." Annika's snide reminder that Katy wasn't in the world trying to teach people floated through her memory, so she added, "We're to fill our minds with whatever is true, honest, just, pure, lovely, or of good report. The television brings too many worldly ideas into a person's head, so we don't watch it."

"Not even cartoons or a how-to show?" Cora raised her eyebrows. "I mean, there's some really cool stuff on TV that isn't, like, crude or sexy or whatever." She turned a hopeful look on Shelby. "Maybe we could watch one of those cooking shows and make what they're cooking. That'd be fun!"

Shelby shook her head. "Nope. Kathleen's dad said no TV."

"Well, how would he know? I mean, it's not like he's here to see." Jewel's tone turned belligerent. She grabbed the movie case from Shelby and opened it. "I want to watch this movie."

"Not tonight." Shelby wrestled the case and disc from Jewel's grasp and handed it to Cora. "Put 'em away. We can spend a fun night without turning on the television."

Jewel flumped back on the couch and folded her arms. "Yeah, right ..."

"How about giving each other manicures and pedicures?" Bridget flipped her hands outward. "I have nail polish in my bag."

"Ooh, great idea!" Cora bounced up and down. "We could do full makeovers! Hair, makeup, nails ... the whole works!"

Shelby tilted her head to the side. "Um ... not so sure that's a good idea."

Cora looked at Katy. Katy offered an apologetic grimace. Cora sighed. "Okay."

"Well ..." Trisha puckered her lips and stared at the ceiling for a moment. "Oh! I know! Let's do a scavenger hunt. We've got enough people to divide into two teams, and we can separate and scour the neighborhood for weird stuff like used toothbrushes or an empty Kleenex box, and whoever finds everything on the list first— "

Shelby held up both hands and waved them back and forth. "Wait, wait ..."

Trisha jutted her chin forward. "What?"

"Kathleen's dad said she's supposed to stay here at the house. So we can't go running around the neighborhood."

Jewel huffed loudly. "Oh, for ..." She glared at Katy. "Why do you have to be such a— "

"Jewel!" Shelby jumped to her feet. "Look ..." Her gaze swept across all of the girls. "We are six intelligent, creative, free-thinking females. Surely we can fill one evening in my house doing activities that won't get Kathleen into trouble with her dad. Now, c'mon, you guys ... think!"

Silence fell. And lengthened. Katy grew more uncomfortable by the minute. Should she ask Shelby's dad to take her home so the others could have fun without her? Just as she was ready to ask the question, Trisha sat up, her face brightening.

"How about a Ping-Pong tournament?"

Jewel crinkled her face. "Ping-Pong ...? That's so lame."

But Cora squealed. "Oh, that was a blast at summer youth night at church! Yeah, let's do it!"

Shelby turned to Katy. "Have you ever played Ping-Pong?"

Katy shook her head.

"Do you think your dad would mind?"

Jewel huffed again, but everyone ignored her.

Katy offered a slow shrug. "It's just a game, right? I don't think he'd mind."

"We do have to go over to the church," Shelby said, "but it's right next door. That won't get you in trouble, will it?"

Jewel threw her arms wide. "Hell-*o*. C'mon, people, her dad's nowhere around. Why are we all so worried about what *he* thinks? We could strip naked and dance in the street and he'd never know!"

Cora, Bridget, and Trisha gawked at Jewel. Shelby's jaw dropped, and she exclaimed, "Jewel!"

Before she could stop herself, Katy said, "If we dance naked in the street, he'll know. We Mennonites *do* read the newspaper, and something that spectacular would definitely make the news."

Dead silence reigned for a moment, and then the room

erupted with screams of laughter. Shelby captured Katy in a hug. Cora laughed so hard tears ran from her eyes. Trisha and Bridget sagged into each other's arms. Everyone roared, except for Jewel, who gave Katy the snootiest, most squinty-eyed look she'd ever seen.

But those few minutes of shared frivolity were worth being glared at by Jewel. Because in those laughter-filled moments, Katy *belonged*.

Chapter Eleven

"Good-bye, Mr. Nuss. Thank you for the ride."

"You're very welcome, Kathleen." Shelby's dad smiled broadly, his eyes warm. "You feel free to visit our house anytime."

Shelby gave Katy a quick hug. "Yeah, anytime—I had a blast. Who would've guessed you'd be such a pro at Ping-Pong? We *stomped* Jewel and Cora."

Katy grinned. She wouldn't have imagined picking up the game so quickly either, but she couldn't remember the last time she'd had so much fun. She'd go to Shelby's every Friday night if her dad would let her. With reluctance, she opened the door and tugged her backpack out with her. "I'll see you at school Monday, Shelby."

"Sure thing, Kathleen! See ya!" Shelby waved through the window as the car pulled away.

Katy's backpack bounced against her knees as she crossed the sidewalk and entered Aunt Rebecca's shop. Two Mennonite women stood with Aunt Rebecca at the fabric-cutting table, and they glanced back when the little bell above the door tinkled. Katy recognized Caleb Penner's mother and aunt. His mother smiled.

"Well, Katy, we were just talking about you. Your aunt says you're making friends at that school in Salina."

Aunt Rebecca probably made the comment as an admonition, but Mrs. Penner's tone carried no reprimand. Katy offered a shy smile. "Yes, ma'am. With some very nice girls. I stayed with them last night. That's why I'm late."

"And there's plenty to do." Aunt Rebecca looked at Katy over her glasses, which perched on the end of her nose. "We nearly sold out on quilt kits during the festival, so I'd like to start restocking."

"Okay. I'll put my backpack away and get started." She headed for the storage room, but Mrs. Penner stopped her.

"Katy, next weekend there will be a corn shucking and singing in our barn." Mrs. Penner smiled, hiding a few freckles with her dimples. "You're more than welcome to come."

Katy swung her backpack, heat building in her ears. A shucking party held a dual purpose—it gave the young people of the community a chance to get together and socialize, and it readied the dry ears to be shelled for animal feed. Annika and Katy had looked forward to the day they were old enough to be invited to one of the young people's gatherings. But now that the chance was offered, dread settled like a stone in her stomach. She didn't know what to say.

Mrs. Penner added in a hopeful tone, "I know Caleb would like you to come, but he's too bashful to ask you himself."

How could Katy gracefully tell this kind woman she had no desire to spend time in her son's company? "Oh. Well. Thank you, Mrs. Penner. I'll ask Dad." *Or maybe I'll forget. Sometimes I forget . . .* "Excuse me, now. I have work to do." She hurried into the back room.

✣

Katy placed the last plate on the shelf in Gramma Ruthie's cupboard and closed the door with a sigh of relief. Task done! Gramma Ruthie, Grampa Ben, and their widowed neighbor, Mrs. Stoltzfus, still sat at the dining room table, sipping coffee and visiting. Even though Katy wasn't a child anymore — graduating from the Schellberg school meant she could sit at the adult table and participate in adult conversation — she had chosen to wash dishes instead of visit.

Whenever she spent time in the company of any of the town's widows, she couldn't help but wonder whether her father might someday court the woman. Dad had been alone a long time — twelve years. She didn't know of any other widows or widowers who had waited so long to remarry. Now that Katy was older, she understood how badly Dad had been hurt when her mother left, so his aching heart probably kept him from wanting to marry again. Or maybe he was just too busy with the cows to court a woman. Either way, being around any of the widows left her feeling edgy, so she didn't mind washing dishes.

But now that the dishes were done, she could get started on her homework. Spending the night at Shelby's and working at Aunt Rebecca's hadn't left much time for class assignments. Dad didn't complain when she did homework on Sunday, but she knew he preferred she honor the Sabbath as a day of rest, just as the Bible advised. So she needed to get as much done before bedtime as possible.

Katy pulled out her books and scattered them across the small table in the middle of Gramma's neat kitchen. Voices filtered in from the dining room, the tones light and cheerful. Katy smiled. With just her and Dad at their house, she was accustomed to mooing cows and whistling wind in the background instead of voices. She found it comforting, listening to the soft hum of conversation.

If Dad were married, would he talk to his wife more than he talked to Katy? Dad was always so quiet. Mrs. Stoltzfus wasn't quiet, though — she'd had plenty to say during dinner, and it didn't sound like she was going to stop talking any time soon. A long time ago, Katy wondered if Dad would court Mrs. Stoltzfus. The woman's husband had passed away shortly after Katy's mother died. She had two sons, both a few years older than Katy, and the community had murmured about how much the boys needed a father. So Katy had asked her dad if he wanted to marry Mrs. Stoltzfus and be a father to Curtis and Steven. She could still see the surprise on Dad's face. He'd spluttered, "Katy-girl, marrying is a subject best left to grown-ups."

Looking back, she was glad Dad hadn't married Mrs. Stoltzfus. It hadn't occurred to her until much later that if Dad was a father to her boys, Mrs. Stoltzfus would be a mother to Katy. And Katy didn't want to call Mrs. Stoltzfus *Mom*. She frowned, realizing she couldn't even remember calling her own mother Mom; she'd left when Katy was so young. If she couldn't call her real mother by that name, then she didn't want to use it on anyone else.

A burst of laughter carried through the dining room door, and Katy glanced over her shoulder. For a moment she considered pouring herself a cup of coffee and joining her grandparents, but then she looked again at the stack of books. *This homework won't finish itself. Stop daydreaming and get busy.*

Sucking in a big breath, she picked up her assignment sheet. She always did her least favorite subject—biology—first to get it out of the way. She groaned when she saw *Chapter review* on the list. That would take at least an hour! With a sigh, she reached into her backpack for notebook paper. Another groan left her lips when she realized her packet of notebook paper was empty. She had lots of paper at home, but that didn't help her at Gramma's house. She needed to write on *something*.

"Gramma must have writing paper in the house ..." She checked each of the drawers in the kitchen, but the only paper she found was a small pad with an advertisement for chicken feed across the top. Stepping into the dining room doorway, she waited until Mrs. Stoltzfus finished talking before calling, "Gramma Ruthie?"

"What is it, Katy-girl?"

Katy offered an apologetic smile for interrupting the conversation. "I need some paper for my homework. Do you have something I could use?"

Mrs. Stoltzfus's eyebrows shot up. "Homework ... That school keeps you busy, hmm?"

Katy didn't particularly care for the way the woman said *that school*, as if it was a place Katy shouldn't go. And why would it be Mrs. Stoltzfus's business anyway? She swallowed her protest and said, "Yes, ma'am, it does."

Mrs. Stoltzfus looked at Gramma and shook her head. "I don't know what Samuel was thinking, sending his daughter to a public high school. Heaven only knows what kinds of habits she'll pick up there. I'd think he'd have more sense, considering what happened with— "

Grampa Ben cleared his throat.

Mrs. Stoltzfus frowned, but she picked up her coffee cup and sipped instead of finishing her sentence. But she didn't need to finish it. Katy knew what she planned to say. *My school isn't any of your business, and neither is my mother!* She wished she could say the words out loud, but being disrespectful would only prove the woman right—that somehow Katy was picking up bad habits. So she bit down on the tip of her tongue and remained silent.

Gramma Ruthie said kindly, "Katy, there's some paper in the drawer in my bedside table. Take what you need."

"Thank you." Katy scuttled through the dining room and into Gramma and Grampa's bedroom. The voices picked up again at the table, but Katy didn't find the sound soothing anymore. She muttered, "I'm *really* glad Dad didn't marry that woman ..." Frowning, she yanked open the drawer and lifted out a black spiral-bound notebook. The first half of the book was filled with Gramma Ruthie's slanted handwriting, so she flipped clear to the back and removed several pages.

She started to put it back in the drawer, but suddenly curiosity got the better of her. Why did Gramma keep this notebook beside the bed? Almost feeling like a burglar, she cracked it open and peeked at a page.

Summer lilacs, scented and bright,
Fill my heart with pure delight ...

Katy hugged the book to her chest, her heart thudding. Poems! Gramma writes poems! She glanced over her shoulder to be certain no one watched her, then she opened the book again. She began to read, smiling at Gramma's written remembrance of fishing with her father when she was a little girl.

"Katy-girl, did you find it?" Gramma's voice called.

Katy jerked. "Yes, ma'am! Thank you!" She slammed the book back in the drawer then snatched up the blank sheets of paper and headed for the kitchen. As she passed through the dining room, she flashed Gramma a smile of thanks. Gramma winked in reply.

She sat at the table and picked up her pencil, but somehow she couldn't concentrate on biology. Images of those neatly written pages kept flashing in front of her eyes. Gramma liked to write! Why hadn't she ever said anything? Gramma knew how much Katy liked writing ... But then she remembered how she often waited until Dad was asleep to take out her journal so he wouldn't walk in and accidentally see what she scribbled onto the page. Writing was personal.

Maybe Gramma didn't want anyone to know. Or maybe Gramma had sent Katy to that notebook so Katy could discover the secret. It didn't matter. Just knowing Gramma liked words and writing made Katy's heart patter. *Someone* in Schellberg understood her desire to write. The realization excited her, and instantly Katy felt less alone—and less weird—than she ever had before.

Chapter Twelve

Katy clipped the last dress onto the clothesline that ran behind the washhouse and a tall fence to keep the clothes concealed from anyone passing on the road. The late September breeze felt crisp and carried a hint of moisture. She'd already washed these clothes — they didn't need a second rinsing from nature. How much simpler life would be if she could toss the wet clothes into an automatic dryer, like the one in Shelby's basement. She pushed that thought aside and scanned the sky for signs of rain.

A few clouds clustered near the horizon in the east, forming a stack of cottonballs. At the sight, her mind began stringing lines together. *Cottonball clouds of snowy white / Set in a cerulean sky / Stretch across vast grassy fields / The colors of Kansas painted high.* Then she shook her head, releasing a little snort. The grassy fields weren't painted high! They hugged the ground. But the poem held promise. She'd have to play with it in her journal tonight.

She picked up the empty wicker basket and headed toward the house. Just as she reached the back stoop, she heard Dad call for her. She put the basket down and ran to the barn. Dad met her in the doorway with a pitchfork in his hand. She took a step backward to avoid running into him.

"Katy, there you are." He glanced at the clothes flapping in the stout breeze. "Laundry all done?"

"Yes, sir. I'm going in now to put supper in the oven. I know I'm starting supper a little late, but— "

Dad shook his head. "Whenever it's ready is fine. I wondered— "

The sound of blasting water intruded, drowning out Dad's words. Caleb Penner was hosing down the floor and walls of the milking room. The high-powered stream pounding against unyielding concrete in the small space resembled an engine's roar. Dad pointed to the yard, and they stepped outside where the racket seemed muffled.

"Why didn't you tell me about Caleb's corn shucking party tonight? He said his mother invited you." A slight scowl creased Dad's face. "I felt embarrassed when Caleb asked if you were coming and I didn't know about it."

She swallowed a frustrated growl. Of course Caleb would ask if she were coming. Who else would he torment if she wasn't there? Katy bit her lower lip. She'd thought about the corn shucking party off and on all week. Being invited was a big deal—it would be her very first party with the community's young people. If only it weren't hosted by Caleb ... A part of her wanted to go, but most of her wanted to avoid time in Caleb Penner's presence, so she hadn't mentioned it to Dad.

"I'm sorry, Dad. I kind of forgot she asked me."

Dad raised one eyebrow. "How can you 'kind of' forget?"

"I'd remember when I wasn't with you, and then ..." Even to her ears, the excuse sounded untruthful. She could hear Jewel's voice: *That's so lame* ... She repeated, "I'm sorry."

"Well, he's a good worker for me, Katy-girl, and he'll be disappointed if you don't go. All the other young people from Schellberg will be there." Dad stuck the pitchfork's tines against the ground and wrapped both fists around the handle. "It would do you good to spend some time with the Schellberg young people."

Katy knew he meant he preferred she not spend so much time with the kids from school. But she couldn't help it—she was in class with them all day long! She pointed to the lines of shirts, trousers, and dresses. "I need to finish the laundry."

"They'll dry just fine without you here, and I can take the things off the line and put them in the kitchen for you."

She couldn't think of any other excuses. She sighed. "All right. I'll go. But I need to get supper in the oven first."

"What are you making?"

"Baked pork chops and stuffing. I thought I'd heat those leftover green beans from yesterday too."

Dad lifted the pitchfork and gave a nod. "Sounds good. Make plenty of stuffing, though. Caleb's going to eat with us, and then you can ride to his house with him."

She opened her mouth to protest.

"It will save me a trip."

She closed her mouth. She wouldn't inconvenience Dad. But she'd make it clear to Caleb the only reason she was going was to please Dad. It had nothing to do with wanting to spend time with *him*.

Caleb pulled the car between the Penners' house and the barn. He hadn't spoken a word on the drive from Katy's farm to his parents' place, which suited Katy fine. She'd had enough trouble being hospitable at the dinner table with Dad looking on. She would please Dad by being a friendly hostess in her own kitchen, but she didn't see any reason to talk to Caleb when Dad wasn't there.

Caleb turned off the ignition and Katy reached for the door handle. She glanced across the grounds. No other cars filled the yard. Nervousness attacked her midsection. She forgot all about not talking to Caleb. "Where is everybody? I thought this was supposed to be a party."

Caleb cleared his throat. "It was. I mean, it is. The others, they'll be comin'."

Katy huffed an irritated breath. Caleb had made it all the way through the ninth grade. Couldn't he form an intelligent sentence? What did Annika see in the dimwitted, freckle-faced boy? "When will they be here?"

"Around eight."

"Eight?" Katy yelped the word. "But that's almost an hour away!"

A sly grin lifted one corner of Caleb's mouth. "I know."

Katy yanked the door handle and swung the door wide. She bounded out of the car, and Caleb scrambled out the other side. Katy crossed her arms and glared at him across the car's roof. "Why didn't you tell my dad that the party starts at eight? He wouldn't have sent me so early if he'd known."

Caleb held his hands outward. His innocent pose didn't fool Katy. The stupid grin gave him away. "I thought he knew. Corn shuckings always start at eight."

Did they? Katy wasn't sure. She huffed again. "Well, what am I supposed to do here by myself for a whole hour?"

Caleb raised one shoulder in a shrug that matched his lopsided grin. "Help my mom with the refreshments?"

Katy rolled her eyes. "Oh, doesn't *that* sound like fun ..." Suddenly she realized she was behaving just like Jewel at school. Her ears started to burn with embarrassment. She didn't like Caleb—he annoyed her more than anyone else she knew—but being mean to him wasn't right either. She started to apologize, but he gestured to his dirty clothes.

"I gotta get cleaned up. Mom's probably in the kitchen. Go on in, Katydid."

She swallowed her apology when he called her the irritating nickname from school. Spinning on her heel, she charged to the house with Caleb behind her. The Penners' brick ranch-style house looked modern and fancy compared to Katy's century-old two-story house. Mr. Penner had built the house when Caleb and Katy were second-graders. Katy recalled Caleb bragging about his new house until Miss Yoder made him memorize Scripture about humility. She'd thought it a well-deserved punishment back then. She wished she had the authority to make Caleb memorize Scripture about not teasing people.

Caleb opened the back door, and they entered a bright, cheerful kitchen. He raced past her and slipped through a doorway on the opposite side of the room. His mother turned from the sink where she was washing her hands. A surprised smile lit her face.

"Why, it's Katy Lambright! I'm so glad you came!" She glanced at a ticking clock that hung on the wall. "You're early."

Katy wrung her hands. "I know. I rode over with Caleb. He thought I might be able to help you with the refreshments."

Mrs. Penner laughed, shaking her head. The black ribbons of her cap swayed beneath her chin, and she shot a tender look toward the doorway where Caleb had disappeared. "Oh, that boy ... Putting one of his guests to work! What is he thinking?" But her tone indicated she wasn't upset at all. She caught Katy's arm and drew her fully into the room. "I suppose I could use the help, if you don't mind."

Katy discovered she didn't mind. Mrs. Penner was such a kind woman. Why couldn't Caleb be more like his mom? "What can I do?"

"Would you get started on the popcorn?" Mrs. Penner pointed to a small appliance with a hooded top that sat in the middle of the kitchen table.

"What is that?" Katy peeked inside the hood.

Mrs. Penner laughed. "Why, that's a popcorn popper, Katy. Caleb and his father bought it for me for my birthday."

Katy scratched her head. At home, she made popcorn in a kettle on the stove. "I don't know how this thing works."

"Well, let me show you. It's very easy."

After receiving instructions on how to operate the popcorn machine, Katy began popping batches of corn. The smell of fresh popcorn, even though she'd eaten a good supper, made her mouth water. She sneaked a few nibbles between batches, earning a grin from Mrs. Penner. When she'd filled four big bowls with white, puffy kernels, she turned off the machine. Her ears continued to ring in the silence that followed.

Mrs. Penner added melted butter and salt to each big bowl while Katy stirred the kernels with a wooden spoon. Katy glanced over to the counter. Plates of cookies, homemade candies, and finger sandwiches formed a neat line. On another countertop, the biggest platter Katy had ever seen held artfully arranged fresh vegetables circling a bowl of speckled dip. Mrs. Penner had gone to a lot of trouble to make sure the young people who attended Caleb's corn shucking were well fed.

Katy carried the wooden spoon to the sink and rinsed it. She looked again at the mountain of food and shook her head. "You sure have plenty for us to eat!"

Mrs. Penner laughed softly. She arranged the four bowls into a square at the edge of the table. "Caleb informed me the food is important for a successful corn shucking party." Her brow crinkled as she looked at Katy. "Do you think there's enough? What's been served at other parties?"

Katy wiped her hands on a towel beside the sink and shrugged. "I don't know. This is my first party."

Mrs. Penner's eyes flew wide. "It is? You haven't been to other shucking parties?"

"No, ma'am." Katy toyed with a ribbon from her cap. "Dad wanted me to wait until I was sixteen before I started attending any of the gatherings. So ..." She flipped her hands outward and grinned. "This is my first."

"Well, now ..." Mrs. Penner stepped close and fluffed the attached cape on Katy's dress. Warmth filled Katy's chest at the unexpected, motherly touch. "How nice that your first party is Caleb's party." She tipped forward, lowering her voice. "You probably already know this, but he's rather sweet on you."

Caleb? Sweet on *her*? The pleasant warmth of moments ago fired from her chest to her ears, becoming an uncomfortable fire. Katy fidgeted.

The woman chuckled. "I've taken you by surprise, haven't I? But rest assured, if Caleb finds a red ear of corn in that pile tonight, he'll probably try to steal a kiss from you."

"Mom!"

At the startled outburst, both Katy and Mrs. Penner turned around. Caleb stood in the kitchen's doorway. His face was as red as Katy's ears had ever been.

Chapter Thirteen

The sound of rubber tires on gravel, slamming car doors, and voices carried through the open window. Katy gestured toward the door, thankful for the distraction. "Caleb's guests are arriving. Do you want the food carried out to the barn?"

Caleb charged past them and out the door. The screen banged hard behind him. Mrs. Penner scowled after him for a moment, then fixed Katy with a smile. "Yes, Katy, we do want the food out in the barn. Thank you for helping."

Katy circled her arms around two bowls of popcorn and headed outside. In the Penners' yard, Schellberg's unmarried youth from late teens to early twenties poured out of pickups and sedans. They stood in groups and laughed and talked, the boys shoving one another's shoulders in fun and the girls leaning close to chat. In some ways, the scene reminded Katy of the high school yard before the bell rang. But the abundance of dresses, little white caps, and flat-brimmed black hats made it clear that this was a Mennonites-only party.

Katy spotted Annika and her sister Taryn with Taryn's beau, Ron Knepp. Katy's feet slowed. She hadn't talked to Annika since the Sunday after Annika and Shelby had spent the night. Her stomach did a funny flip-flop. Would Annika ignore her or spend time with her this evening?

Suddenly Annika turned and her eyes collided with Katy's. Her shoulders jerked, as if someone poked her, and then she walked slowly to meet Katy. "I didn't see your dad's pickup. When did you get here?" Annika took one of the popcorn bowls and together they moved toward the barn.

How should Katy respond? It seemed Annika was willing to forget their disagreement. But if she confessed Caleb had driven her to his house, would Annika's friendliness disappear again? "I got here early," she said. Even though she hadn't lied, her conscience still pricked. "Mrs. Penner has lots of food to carry out. Would you help me?"

The girls made several trips along with Caleb's mother to deliver all of the plates, platters, and bowls of food to a long table set up in the barn. At the end of the table on the dirt floor, bottles of root beer and lemonade floated in a big iron tub of ice. Annika pulled out a bottle of root beer and wiped the glass on her skirt before opening the top. She took a long swig and grinned. "All this food looks great, doesn't it? I wonder what activities Caleb has planned."

Katy shrugged. "What do they usually do at corn shuckings?"

Annika laughed. "Shuck corn! And sing. And eat." She looked again at the table of food. "Think it would be okay to get started? Those little sandwiches look really good."

Katy stifled a giggle. Annika and food ... When she was eating, she was happy. "Might want to grab them before the boys start filling their plates. The food will be gone in no time!"

Annika picked up a plate. Apparently her action signaled that it was time to eat, because the guests swarmed the table. Mrs. Penner's beautifully arranged plates and platters held only crumbs by the time the older boys cleared away from the table. Katy managed to snag two finger sandwiches, several carrot sticks, and a cookie. Ron Knepp stepped past Katy to retrieve a bottle of root beer.

She looked longingly at his overflowing plate of goodies and sighed. "I guess there's a good reason not to invite boys to a party. They eat too much."

Annika giggled, throwing a smile at three boys who dug through the ice for bottles of root beer. "But what's a party without boys?"

Katy nearly rolled her eyes. She steered Annika a few feet away from the ravaged table. "Sometimes it can be fun to have just girls. At Shelby's house, we— "

Annika's eyes narrowed.

Katy clacked her teeth together to hold back any other words. After a moment of tense silence, she said, "Looks like the boys are getting ready to start shucking. Should we go watch? I think Lucas Bornholdt will shuck the most ears." Annika didn't move. Katy added impulsively, "Caleb will come in last."

Annika jerked to life. "Caleb won't come in last! I think he'll keep up ear-for-ear with the older boys."

Katy grinned. "Let's go find out."

The two girls cheered and giggled along with the older girls as the boys zipped through bushels of dry ears of corn. Shucks flew, raising dust, and Katy sneezed repeatedly, but she refused to leave the barn. Being elbow to elbow with the other girls in her fellowship, laughing and calling out words of encouragement, filled Katy with a feeling of oneness she didn't want to lose.

Ron Knepp suddenly yelped and held up a red ear

of corn. The wild shucking came to a halt. Some boys groaned. Others slapped Ron on the back and congratulated him. The two girls behind Katy and Annika sucked in their breath, and those on Katy's left clapped wildly and pushed Annika's sister Taryn forward.

Katy knew what the red ear meant—the boy could give a kiss to the girl of his choice. Since Ron and Taryn were published to be married, Ron would surely kiss Taryn. Three years ago, Taryn had come home from a shucking party, pink-faced from receiving her first kiss from Ron. She'd shared every detail with Annika, who in turn had shared every detail with Katy. Annika had seemed enthralled with the idea of being kissed, but Katy had been more appalled than intrigued. Shouldn't kissing be private? She didn't want her first kiss to be in front of a bunch of people in a barn with corn shucks under her feet and dust filling the air. And she didn't want to watch Ron kiss Taryn either.

She turned to move to the back of the group, but a commotion in the circle of boys caught her attention. Two older boys grabbed Caleb and threw him to the center of the shuckers. Ron bowed and handed the red ear of corn to Caleb. "Here ya go, Caleb. It's all yours. Your first party—your first kiss." A whoop rose from the other boys, accompanied by congratulatory slaps on the back. Apparently they'd had this all planned out.

Caleb's freckled face broke into a smug grin. He took the ear and scanned the group of girls. His eyes locked on Katy's. Katy's pulse began to pound. She wanted to flee, but Annika gripped Katy's elbow. Her fingers dug in deep, and Katy couldn't move.

Caleb tapped the air with the red ear and advanced

slowly toward the girls, his gaze flitting back and forth between Annika and Katy. Mrs. Penner's words ran through Katy's mind: *He's sweet on you, you know.*

"Hmm," Caleb mused aloud, "should I choose Antarctica or Katydid?"

Those reprehensible nicknames from school! Irritation rose from Katy's middle. She balled her fists and jutted her chin. "Don't even *think* about trying to kiss *me*, Caleb Penner! I'll smack you so hard it'll knock your freckles off!"

Caleb came to an abrupt halt. His eyes widened and his mouth gaped open like a fish gasping for air. The boys slapped their legs and roared. After a moment of stunned silence, the girls also began to laugh.

Taryn slung her arm around Katy's shoulders and shook her finger at Caleb. "Oooh, she told you, Caleb. Better drop that ear of corn and step back!"

Other comments followed, but Katy didn't stick around to listen. She wiggled loose from Taryn's grip and ran from the barn toward the house. The sun had set, and only an electric lamp high on a wooden pole threw out a scant yellow glow. She was forced to slow down or trip in the deep shadows. Halfway across the yard, someone grabbed her arm and turned her around. Even in the dim light, Katy couldn't miss the anger snapping in Annika's eyes.

"Why'd you do that? Yell at him and then run off?" Annika shook Katy's arm. "He said 'Antarctica *or* Katydid.' He might've kissed *me* if you hadn't acted all huffy and made such a big deal out of things."

Katy jerked her arm free. "And he might've kissed *me*. He was coming straight at me. I don't want to be kissed by Caleb Penner!"

"Well, maybe I do!" Annika grabbed her again. "You're

going to a big school where there are lots of boys. Here in Schellberg, how many boys are there our age? One!" Annika thrust her finger in the air and nearly hit Katy in the chin with her fingertip. "Caleb Penner. And now you've chased him off with your snooty actions. What's wrong with you, Katy? Why can't you have fun and be like everybody else? It's just a game! Why do you always have to be so weird?"

Katy pulled away from Annika and backed up several steps. Just because she didn't want Caleb Penner kissing her didn't make her weird. Wasn't she entitled to her own feelings? And why did she and Annika have to fight over everything? They were finally getting along again, and now everything fell apart over a stupid red ear of corn in a shucking game.

"Well, I hope you're happy," Annika went on. She folded her arms over her chest and glared at Katy. "I don't know how I can go back in there and face everybody after you ran off like a big baby."

Katy's nose stung, and she knew she was about to prove Annika right about being a big baby. "I need to use the bathroom," she blurted out and ran for the house. She burst through the porch door, and Mrs. Penner jumped up from the kitchen table.

"Oh, Katy!" The woman placed her hand over her throat. "You startled me." Then she frowned. "Are you all right?"

Katy blinked back tears. "I'm not feeling very well, Mrs. Penner. I think I need to go home."

"Oh, I'm so sorry, honey. I hope it wasn't something you ate." Mrs. Penner bustled forward and patted Katy's shoulder. "You stay right here. I'll go get Caleb and have him— "

"No!" Katy almost yelled the word.

Mrs. Penner jumped back.

Katy shook her head. "I mean, he's having fun with his friends. I don't want him to have to leave. Maybe I can just ... walk home." It was only five miles or so.

"Oh no you won't! Not in the dark." Mrs. Penner guided Katy to the table and pushed her into a chair. "You sit here and rest. I'll go get Mr. Penner and have him run you home." She hurried out of the room before Katy could reply.

A few minutes later, Mr. Penner walked Katy to his pickup truck. Happy sounds came from the barn—laughter and singing. An odd feeling welled up inside of Katy. Part of her wanted to hurry home, escape to her bedroom, and climb into her bed, and part of her wanted to return to the barn and stay for the rest of the party. She paused beside the truck. "Mr. Penner ...?"

"Yeah?"

Then Annika's words returned: *Why do you always have to be so weird?* Did the others think she was weird too, for running off that way? Suddenly she didn't want to know. "Nothing. Never mind. I'm ready to go." She didn't look back as Mr. Penner started the engine and turned the truck toward the road.

Chapter Fourteen

Katy tossed the covers aside and crept from her bed. She rolled a towel and tucked it along the doorjamb before flipping on her little desk lamp. She didn't want any light sneaking under the door and alerting Dad that she was still awake. He'd sent her straight to bed when Mr. Penner delivered her home, assuming she must be ill to leave her very first party so early.

Katy was ill, in a way. Not physically ill, but heartsick. Her chest ached like a bad tooth. Confusion rolled through her, and she needed to sort out her thoughts. She sat at her desk and pulled her journaling notebook and pencil from the drawer. But then she just sat, pencil poised above the page, unable to capture her thoughts and put them into words.

Images from the two parties she'd attended — the one at Shelby's, and the one at Caleb's — flashed in her memory. She intentionally drew on cheerful moments from each: batting the Ping-Pong ball across the table while Trisha and Cora cheered, standing elbow to elbow with the Mennonite girls and cheering for the boys who shucked corn, lying on her stomach and whispering late into the night with Shelby and Bridget, and talking with Mrs. Penner as they stirred butter and salt into the popcorn.

Then two very strong, opposite remembrances battled for prominence: Shelby hugging Katy after she made the teasing comment about dancing in the streets, and Annika grabbing her arm and accusing her of ruining the party. Confusion made Katy's head ache. She was Mennonite. Shouldn't the happiest memory come from her time with her Mennonite friends instead of with Shelby, a worldly girl?

She didn't want to be like her mother, drawn from her community of faith into the world. Yet the hurtfulness of Annika's harsh words made her want to escape to a different place ... She shifted to look out her bedroom window at the gray late-evening sky, and the gently swaying branches of the tall pin oak between the house and barn caught her attention. Nearly all of the leaves had fallen already, but her eyes focused on one lonely leaf dangling from the tip of a slim branch.

Katy pressed the pencil's point to the paper and words began to flow.

A single leaf clings to the tree;
On branches bare it dares to be.
Maintaining, alone, its tenuous hold
While threatened by a wind, so cold.
On the ground below so many leaves
Look up and challenge, "Come with me.
Why hang there, friendless and alone?
Come with us—just let go!"
The last leaf moans and holds so tight—
It won't give up without a fight.
The wind comes stronger, pulling hard ...

Her heart pounded so hard, her hand shook. How should the poem end? Would she hold tight to her bonds within the Mennonite community, or would Shelby's acceptance, warmth, and friendliness draw Katy away? Her fingers gripped the pencil, and she wrote the final line in wobbly letters:

The last leaf falls upon the yard.

Katy put her head on her desk and began to cry.

Sunday morning, Katy stumbled into the kitchen wearing her nightgown and robe. Her head throbbed from last night's crying, and a look in the little mirror that hung above the sink made her groan. Red, puffy eyes peered back at her from beneath tangled hair. If she had some of that makeup from Cora's bag, she might be able to make herself look presentable for worship. Not that showing up at the meetinghouse with makeup would be considered presentable.

Katy sighed and pulled the cast iron frying pan from its shelf. She'd better get Dad's breakfast made. Before she could break eggs into the skillet, Dad stepped through the back door with a full milk jug in his hand. He stopped when he spotted Katy. His eyebrows formed a deep V.

"Katy-girl, are you still sick? I thought you'd feel better after a good night's rest."

Katy hadn't gotten a good night's rest. She smoothed her hair with her hand and yawned. "I'm sorry, Dad."

He shook his head. "Well, just fix me some oatmeal for breakfast, then go back to bed." He put the milk jug in the refrigerator and headed for the stairs.

Katy watched him go, an intense longing making her chest feel tight. If she had a mother, surely she'd be tucked tenderly into bed with a cool cloth on her forehead to ease her headache. But Dad expected her to fix breakfast and tuck herself in. He seemed more aggravated than sympathetic. Tears threatened again. She sniffed hard and reminded herself he was willing to let her stay home instead of going to service. She couldn't ever remember missing service when she wasn't really, really sick.

As quickly as possible, she prepared a pot of oatmeal, adding raisins and cinnamon the way Dad liked it. Just as she set the finished oatmeal at the back of the stove to keep it warm, Dad entered the room, dressed in his dark suit and white shirt for service. He spooned gloppy oatmeal into the bowl and sent her a puzzled look over his shoulder. "Are you going to eat?"

Her stomach spun. She shook her head.

"Then go back to bed, Katy-girl. You need to be better by tomorrow so you won't miss school too."

Katy scuttled toward the staircase, leaving Dad alone. Halfway up the stairs, she paused and listened to the clink of Dad's spoon against his bowl. She envisioned him sitting at the table alone. A funny lump filled her throat. Did Dad ever pine for his lost wife the way Katy longed for her lost mother? She wished she had the courage to ask, but she knew better than to talk about her mom. Dad's mouth always went into a firm line when her name was mentioned. She'd better keep her thoughts to herself.

Back in her bedroom, she retrieved her journal and pencil and burrowed under the covers. She intended to record her thoughts, but the warm, comfortable bed lulled her to sleep.

The next thing she knew someone knocked on her door, waking her. She sat up and called, "Come in."

Gramma Ruthie stepped into the room. Her wrinkled face pursed with concern. "Katy-girl, your dad says you're sick."

Happiness welled up and spilled over in two tears. "Oh, Gramma Ruthie, I'm so glad you're here!"

Gramma bustled forward and perched on the edge of Katy's bed. She ran her hand over Katy's forehead. Katy closed her eyes and leaned into the touch. Gramma's cool, smooth hand felt so good. "No fever ... Are you throwing up?"

"No."

"Throat hurt?"

"No, ma'am."

Gramma clasped her hands in her lap. "So what's wrong?"

Katy flumped back against her pillows. "I don't know, Gramma. I just ..." Her words fell away. She couldn't confess her deepest fears. Gramma had already suffered with Dad when Katy's mother ran away. It wouldn't be fair to make Gramma worry about Katy following her mother's example.

For several minutes Gramma sat and looked into Katy's face, waiting in silence. Then she squeezed Katy's knee. "You're not really sick, are you, Katy-girl?"

Katy's chin started to quiver. She clamped her teeth together.

"You're just feeling ... a little lost and confused?"

Very slowly, she nodded her head.

Gramma chuckled. "Ah, Katy-girl, I suspected this would happen when you were allowed to go to that high school. But I didn't think it would happen so soon. I should have known better. You're too curious to let anything be for long."

Katy wriggled to sit up higher. She leaned toward Gramma. "Did you ever feel lost and confused?"

Gramma's eyes twinkled. "Does a chicken have feathers?"

Katy grinned.

"I think every young person goes through a time of wondering." Gramma rested her palm on the bed. Suddenly her forehead crinkled and she tapped her knuckles on the spot where her hand had landed. A muffled thud sounded. Katy quickly reached beneath the blankets and pulled out her journal.

With a puzzled expression, Gramma held out her hand. Katy started to hug the notebook to her chest in refusal, but then she remembered Gramma's journal. If anyone would understand Katy's need to pour her feelings onto paper, surely Gramma would. And maybe the words on the page could tell Gramma how Katy was feeling. She flipped it open to where she'd written the poem about the leaf. "W-would you read my poem?"

Gramma didn't even blink. She nodded soberly and then bent her head over the page, her white ribbons swaying above Katy's lines of print. Her lips moved silently as she read. And then she gave Katy a tender look. "Are you the leaf, Katy-girl, being pulled from the tree?"

Katy couldn't answer. Her heart pounded. Would Gramma be disappointed in her for even thinking about being tugged away from the faith of her family and community?

Gramma closed the notebook and sighed. "Did you know that the Amish people have something called *rumspringa*, where they let the young people have a time of ... well, running around?"

Katy had heard the word, but since it wasn't practiced in her faith, she hadn't paid much attention. She shook her head.

"It's a way for the kids to get all the restlessness and worldliness out of their systems before joining the church," Gramma explained. "Every young person is curious about the world. I don't know whether I approve of the rum-springa or not—maybe it's good to let the kids see both sides so they know for sure what they're choosing when they join the church, and maybe it's just allowing them to roll in sinfulness. But I do know that a person needs to enter willingly into faith or it's not a faith of freedom, but bondage. Does that make sense to you?"

Katy tipped her head. "I think so. But, Gramma, I already joined the church. I don't *want* to drift away." Tears filled her eyes. She gave the moisture an impatient flick with her fingers.

Gramma smiled and squeezed Katy's knee again. "And that's exactly why you're not feeling good, my girl. Because your flesh and your spirit are at war with each other."

Katy opened her journal again and read the last line of her poem. *The last leaf falls upon the yard.* She swallowed. The words seemed ominous. "So how do I make sure the spirit wins?"

"How?" Gramma clicked her tongue on her teeth, her eyes twinkling. "Well, Katy-girl, you already know how. You trust God to give you the strength you need to rise above temptation. What does the Bible teach us? God will not allow you to be tempted beyond what you can bear."

"But, Gramma ..." Katy's mouth went dry. She leaned forward and lowered her voice to a whisper. "My mom. She ..." She licked her lips. "She went away. Away from Dad, away from me, away from the church. Temptation got control of her. What if ..." Katy couldn't bring herself to ask the question.

Gramma took both of Katy's hands. Tears winked in her eyes. "God always provides a way out, darling girl, but it's up to you to take it. Choose wisely, my Katy. Choose wisely ..."

Chapter Fifteen

Choose wisely ... Gramma Ruthie's words followed Katy to school on Monday. When kids goofed off in biology and Katy was tempted to giggle in response, she turned her attention to her work instead. On Tuesday in the cafeteria, several students began chanting, "Meatloaf sucks! Meatloaf sucks!" Katy wholeheartedly agreed — the school cooks could learn a thing or two from Gramma Ruthie. But before she got caught up in joining the throng, she remembered her grandmother's words and chose to scrape her uneaten portion into the trash can and leave the cafeteria.

Wednesday morning she waited outside the doors for the bell to ring, as had become her routine. She missed Shelby, who was already inside with the others who came early for Bible study. Katy wished she could join them, but the rule stated you came on time or you couldn't come at all. Being a bus rider, she couldn't make it on time, so she stood outside alone. Much to Katy's surprise, Jewel sauntered up and leaned against the window.

"Hey, Kathleen. How's it goin'?"

Katy flicked a quick glance at Jewel. The girl always looked either bored or snooty. This morning she wore her bored face. Katy preferred it to the squinty-eyed glare Jewel had perfected. "All right, I guess. How are you?"

Jewel snorted. "Oh, I'm just great. I'm livin' with a bunch of Bible-thumpin', church-pushin' goody-goodies who are about to drive me over the edge with their big smiles and constant hugs." She rolled her eyes, and her lips curled into a snarl. "I can't wait to get back home again. Won't be long now ..."

Katy stared at Jewel in amazement. Shelby hadn't said much, but what little she had revealed made Katy believe Jewel would be delighted to be away from her unpleasant home. "Really?"

Jewel shot her an impatient look. "Yes, *really*. I mean, get real. There are more rules at the Nuss house than you've probably got in your old-fashioned church. *Don't* swear, *don't* stay out late, *don't* wear tight clothes. Don't, don't, don't!" Jewel's voice rose. "Then there are the stupid do's — *do* your homework, *do* your chores, *do* get up early on Sunday for church. I never get a minute's peace!" Jewel swore softly, shaking her head. "They're so stupid. Like they're gonna change me or something ..." Jewel tossed her head, making her long, dyed red hair bounce. She announced dramatically, "I am who I am."

Katy examined the stubborn jut to Jewel's jaw. She braved a question. "Do you miss your mom?"

"Well, *duh*." Jewel gawked at Katy. "Wouldn't you?" Then she snorted again. "Oh, yeah, I forgot. Shelby said your mom's dead. Sorry." She didn't sound sorry. A dreamy smile lifted the corners of Jewel's mouth. "My mom's totally cool. She lets me do whatever I want to, whenever I want to. *So* unlike the Nusses." Her shoulders heaved a huge sigh. "I don't know why the stupid social worker had to stick her big nose into our lives. We were just fine."

Katy knew that the children who came to live with Miss Albrecht in Schellberg at a social worker's insistence weren't "just fine." They'd either been neglected or mistreated and desperately needed someone to care for them. She couldn't imagine why Jewel would be taken from her home if things were safe for her, but she sensed it was better not to explore the reasons.

"What about your dad?"

Jewel's eyes scrunched. "What about him?"

"Do you miss him too?"

Jewel crossed her arms over her chest and stared across the yard. "Don't know him. He was outta my life before I was born."

Katy flinched. She knew how it felt not to know a parent. She hadn't had a chance to get to know her mother. Not really. She touched Jewel's arm. "I'm sorry, Jewel. It must be hard for you to be away from your mom — especially since she's all you've got."

Jewel stared at Katy for a moment as if confused. Then she shrugged, and her expression hardened. "Yeah, well, I'll survive." She rolled her eyes again. "If I can live with the Nuss nuts, I can survive anything." She yawned. "Man, I'd love to skip out today and just sleep the day away ..." Suddenly she grabbed Katy's arm and pulled her behind the tall cedar trees that grew on either side of the school's doors. She leaned close, her eyes snapping. "Kathleen, wanna have some fun?"

Katy licked her lips, nervous. "Like what?"

"Like taking off. Goin' somewhere. We could take a

city bus or a taxi to my mom's place. She's always got good snacks in the cupboard—not the healthy stuff Mrs. Nuss keeps in the house." Jewel made a face, and then she waggled her eyebrows. "It'd be great. A day of no school, no rules, just hangin' out and doin' what we want to. How 'bout it?"

Katy's stomach turned a funny flip-flop. *Choose wisely, my Katy.* "I don't know, Jewel ..."

Jewel huffed. "Come on! Do you always have to be so perfect?"

Do you always have to be so weird? Annika's barb flashed through Katy's mind. "I'm not perfect ... and I'm not weird!"

"All right then." Jewel tossed her backpack against the brick wall, well behind the bushes. "Put your stuff there and let's go. We'll be back before the end-of-the-day buzzer so you can catch the bus home."

"But won't we get in trouble?" The school's rule book said kids needed permission from a parent to miss school. She knew Dad wouldn't give her permission to run off with Jewel.

Jewel rolled her eyes and released another mighty huff. "C'mon, Kathleen. Think about it. An entire day of *freedom*."

Katy thought about the Amish rumspringa—the chance to explore. Surely one day wouldn't hurt anything.

Suddenly Jewel let out a mighty sigh. She folded her arms over her chest and gave her squinty-eye look. "I should've known you'd be too much of a goody-goody to do anything fun. Little Miss Perfect ..."

The mocking tone was Katy's undoing. She stomped her foot. "I can too have fun. Let's go." She dropped her backpack next to Jewel's.

Jewel's face broke into a huge smile. "Really?"

"As long as we're back in time for me to catch the bus home." Katy conscience pricked, but she pushed the feeling aside. Jewel needed the company or she wouldn't have invited Katy to come along. She was doing Jewel a favor.

"Great!" Jewel grabbed Katy's arm and herded her toward the far corner of the parking lot. "We're outta here!"

✣

"Thanks, mister." Jewel tossed a ten dollar bill over the seat at the taxi driver then climbed out of the car's backseat. Katy followed and stood at the curb, looking around at the neighborhood. Trepidation made her pulse race. The houses were small and sad looking with peeling paint, broken windows, or trash-strewn yards. Sometimes all three.

Jewel bounded onto the cracked sidewalk and looked back at Katy. "Well, come on."

Katy hesitated. "What is this place?"

Jewel laughed, but it sounded brittle. "This is *home*, girlfriend."

Katy swallowed. Jewel preferred *this* over Shelby's neat house and well-kept lawn? Across the street, a dog started to bark and someone hollered at it to shut up. The dog yelped and then fell silent.

Jewel plunked her fist on her hip. "You gonna stand there all day, or are you comin' in?"

Katy stepped onto the sidewalk. "Which one is yours?"

Jewel charged across a yard of hard-packed dirt with forlorn tufts of dried grass poking up here and there. "This one." She kicked a beer can out of the way and hopped onto the cement square that served as a porch. "Hope

Mom left the door unlocked." She twisted the doorknob, but the door didn't budge. "Locked. Figures." She smacked the door with her palm and then shrugged. "Oh, well. We can get in through the bathroom window. C'mon."

Katy trailed Jewel to the back of the house. Jewel stood on a cinder block and wiggled a window until it screeched upward. "Give me a boost." Automatically, Katy grabbed Jewel's foot, and Jewel pushed off. She fell through the open window then called from inside, "Go to the back door — I'll let you in."

Katy considered returning to the curb and flagging down a taxi. But how would she pay for it? Gramma Ruthie's admonition — *Choose wisely* — ran through her mind. She wished she'd listened to it earlier instead of giving in to Jewel. But now it was too late.

"Kathleen! Where are you?" Jewel sounded aggravated.

Katy trotted around to the back of the house. Jewel held a door open. She gestured for Katy to come in, and a big grin lit her face. "Just like I said — nobody here. We've got the place to ourselves."

An unpleasant odor attacked Katy's nose as she stepped over the threshold. She fought the urge to hold her nose. Dirty dishes with spoiling food littered the countertops, and a trash can in the corner overflowed onto the floor.

Jewel stepped past the mess and started flinging open cabinet doors. "Aw, c'mon, Mom, I know you've got something good somewhere. She always keeps, like, Twinkies or Doritos on hand ... Yeah!" Jewel spun around with a half-empty bag of cheese curls in her hand. "Perfect!"

Katy wrinkled her nose. Cheese curls this early in the morning? Besides, the smell killed any appetite she might have had. But she followed Jewel into a dark, cluttered living room. Jewel threw herself onto the couch and picked up a small box from a scarred end table. "Sit down, Kathleen." She pointed the little box at the television set and pushed a button. The television blared to life.

Katy backed up quickly and stopped in the doorway. From where she stood, she couldn't see the television screen. If she took even one step forward, the picture would be in her line of vision. Her toes twitched inside her sneakers. This was her rumspringa—should she take a peek? Just to see what she was missing?

She tipped her head and listened. She heard some kind of loud argument between a man and a woman, both of whom were using language that made Katy cringe. She inched backward. Maybe listening would be rumspringa enough.

Jewel patted the sofa and opened the bag in her hand. "C'mon, Kathleen. Have some cheese curls and chill out."

"I—I better not."

"You gonna stand there all day? 'Cause the point of skipping school was to relax, right? You can't relax standing up."

"I know, but . . ." Katy flipped her hand toward the television.

Jewel stared at Katy. "Are you really serious about that not watching TV stuff?"

Katy nodded.

"Well, okay then. Suit yourself." Jewel popped a cheese curl in her mouth. "I guess you can go sit in the kitchen. Snoop around for something else to eat, if you want." She wiggled into the sagging couch cushions and aimed her gaze at the television screen.

With a sigh, Katy returned to the kitchen. She pulled out a vinyl-backed chair and sat. The nauseating smells made her stomach churn. Seeing the television had to be better than sitting here, breathing in the awful odor of spoiled food. She rose to join Jewel, but just then the back door slammed open and a man stepped into the kitchen. Lank hair straggled over his ears, and dark whiskers dotted his face. He wore a stretched out T-shirt that didn't quite cover his belly. He looked frightening. Although she wanted to flee, she froze in place as the man locked gazes with her.

He dropped a bulging plastic bag onto the closest counter, kicked the door shut, and hitched up his blue jeans. "Who're you? And how'd you get in here?"

Katy stared at the man, unable to answer.

He stomped forward three steps. "I asked you a question, girl." Then he looked toward the doorway that led to the living room. "You alone here?"

Katy shook her head wildly. Her ribbons slapped against her neck. "I — I'm here with Jewel."

"Jewel?" The man scratched his chin. "That so . . . ?" He ambled through the doorway, and Katy followed him. Jewel glanced over at the man, and her face went white. She sat straight up. The man leaned forward and slapped a button on the TV. Silence fell. Placing his hands on his hips, he grinned at Jewel. "Well if my little Jewelly didn't come home. C'mere, darlin', an' give me a big ol' hug."

Jewel stood, but she didn't move toward the man. Her expression turned sullen. "I'm not your 'little Jewelly,' and I'm not giving you a hug. Why're you here, anyway?"

The man laughed. "I live here, darlin', or did you forget?"

Jewel's jaw dropped. "Y-you live here? But Mom said

she kicked you out! She said she had to or she couldn't get me back!"

"Aw, now, Jewel, you know your mom says lots of things ..." He poked his thumb toward Katy. "So how'd you get hooked up with this little nun?"

"She's not a nun," Jewel snapped, "she's Mennonite. And you leave her alone."

The man gave Katy a head-to-toes-and-up-again look. "I'm not botherin' her." Then he swung toward Jewel again. "But why're you here? That social worker let you go?"

"I came to see Mom." Jewel tossed the bag of cheese curls aside. The contents bounced across the couch seat. She skittered past the man, her narrowed gaze pinned to him and her lips set in a grim line. She pushed Katy toward the back door. "C'mon, Kathleen. Let's go."

Katy didn't hesitate. The girls hurried outside with the man following them. He held the back door open and called after them, "You don't hafta leave, Jewel. Your mom'll be back soon — don't ya wanna stay and see her?"

"No, thanks!" Jewel escorted Katy around the house to the sidewalk. She kept glancing back, her breath coming in little puffs. She didn't slow down until they reached the corner. "Okay," she said, looking left and right before pulling Katy across the street. "There's a park a few blocks over. We can hang out there until this afternoon. Then we'll go back to school."

Katy had to trot to keep up with Jewel. The morning air was cool, and she shivered in spite of her sweater. "Who was that man?"

Jewel grunted. "His name's Hugo. He's my mom's ... boyfriend." Her steps slowed. "I can't believe he's living there. When Mom came to see me last week, she *promised*— " Jewel stopped abruptly. She balled her hands into fists and glared straight ahead. "I shouldn't've believed her. I should've known, but I hoped . . ."

To Katy's surprise, Jewel burst into tears.

Chapter Sixteen

As abruptly as Jewel started to cry, she stopped. Katy had never seen anyone grab control so quickly. Jewel pressed the heels of her hands into her eye sockets, took one shuddering breath, then whisked the tears away.

"Let's get to that park before Hugo decides to come after us. He's not exactly predictable." She grabbed Katy's arm and dragged her along.

Katy stumbled on a crack in the sidewalk, but Jewel didn't slow her pace. They reached a rundown park with a few swings, a warped teeter-totter, and a rusty jungle gym in the middle of a square plot of grassless ground. Jewel ducked under the jungle gym and sat, leaning against one of the metal support bars. Katy didn't want to sit in the dirt, but she decided it would be best to stay near Jewel. So she perched on a climbing rung and folded her hands in her lap. The chill from the iron bar seeped through her skirt and made her shiver. She hunched further into her sweater.

Jewel looked at Katy and laughed. "You look like a little old lady there." She snorted. "Your clothes . . . honestly, call the fashion police! Too bad we couldn't stay at my house. Would've been fun to dig out some of my stuff and dress you. You're actually kind of pretty, even though you hide it with that whacked-out hat and granny dress."

Had Jewel paid her a compliment? "Thanks ..." She criss-crossed her sweater over her body as a cool breeze whisked past. "Are we going to stay here all day?"

Jewel made a face. "I know. It's not what I planned. But Hugo ..." She expelled a puff of breath. "I can't stand that guy."

Katy understood. Her few minutes with Hugo had left her feeling as though bugs crawled under her skin.

"Know what really ticks me off?" Jewel's tone turned hard and her eyes narrowed to slits. "Mom *knows* I can't come home until he's out. Him and me ... he ... We can't be under the same roof. The social worker told Mom, 'Get him out and we can send Jewel home.' But she lets him stay." Jewel gritted her teeth. She turned to stare across the park. "How would you feel if your mom chose something like *him* over you?"

Katy shifted. The iron bar dug into her skin, making her legs tingle. She drew in a breath and whispered, "I know how it feels. My mom ..." She gulped. "My mom left my dad and me. She left me behind."

Jewel shot Katy a startled glance. "Huh?" Then she waved her hand. "Your mom died. That's not the same thing. She didn't *choose* death."

Katy shook her head and slipped off the bar to sit on the ground. She looked into Jewel's face. "My mom died four years *after* she left my dad and me. So she chose something ... or someone ... over me. I just don't know what."

"You're kidding." Jewel bent her legs and rested her elbows on her knees. "She just took off one day? Wow . . ."

Katy nodded. A lump in her throat kept her from saying anything else. For several minutes she and Jewel sat without speaking. Then suddenly Jewel lunged to her feet. She held out her hand. "C'mon, Kathleen. It's no fun sitting out here. And I'm getting cold. I left my jacket at the house when Hugo surprised me. We might as well go back to school."

Katy allowed Jewel to pull her up, then she brushed off the seat of her skirt. "Will we walk back?"

"Nah, I've got money for a taxi." Jewel flashed a grin. "Mrs. Nuss needs to quit leaving her purse open on the table. Makes it too easy for me to help myself."

Katy gawked at Jewel. How could the girl smile while admitting she stole from Shelby's mother?

"Oh, don't look so shocked, Miss Goody-goody." Jewel sauntered down the sidewalk and Katy trotted along beside her. "I learned a long time ago nobody *gives* you anything. You have to take while the taking is good or you end up with nothin'."

The tender moments of shared understanding with Jewel disappeared. Katy clamped her lips shut and chose not to argue. Biblical admonitions cluttered her mind, but she suspected Jewel would just roll her eyes at anything she said. Besides, how could she preach to Jewel about right and wrong when she'd just knowingly left school without permission? The reality of her choices slammed down on her.

They walked several blocks before Jewel flagged down a taxi, and the driver delivered them back to school. Jewel darted behind the bushes and emerged with both backpacks.

Katy took her bag and slipped her arms through the straps while Jewel flung her bag over one shoulder and stood with her weight on one hip, staring across the schoolyard with a bored expression on her face. For some reason, even though they were in the same grade, Katy felt years younger than Jewel. Jewel possessed an arrogant confidence that aged her. The realization made Katy uncomfortable. She started toward the doors, but Jewel caught hold of her bag and pulled her back.

"Wait 'til the next bell rings. We want to go in while people are heading to the cafeteria. That way we can blend in with the crowd."

"So we're going to sneak in?"

Jewel rolled her eyes. "Duh."

Being sneaky was the same as lying—and didn't the Bible teach that deceitfulness always led to trouble? Katy's sins were multiplying. But she stayed with Jewel and waited until the bell rang.

"C'mon." Jewel inched forward, peering furtively through the glass doors. When the hallway was congested with students, she darted forward, opened the door, and sauntered in to join the crowd. Katy followed, her ears burning and her legs quivering. They entered the cafeteria and got in line for a tray. Jewel flashed Katy a grin. "See? Piece o' cake ..."

Just as the girls turned with their trays to find a table, Shelby dashed up to them. "Jewel! *Here* you are. Did Dad find you?"

Jewel scowled. "Whaddaya mean?" She moved toward the nearest table.

Shelby followed with Katy close on her heels. "When you

didn't show up this morning, I went to the office and called Dad. I thought maybe you'd gotten sick or something."

Jewel slammed down her tray and glared at Shelby. "You did *what*?"

"I called Dad," Shelby repeated. She flicked a glance at Katy then faced Jewel again. "I thought maybe you'd gotten sick. But he said he'd dropped you off at school. Where've you been?"

Jewel plunked her backpack into a chair and released a loud huff. "Honestly, Shelby, can't you stay out of my business? I don't need you checking up on me. I don't need you snitching on me." Jewel whirled and stormed away.

Shelby looked at Katy. "I didn't mean to tattle on her. I honestly was worried."

Katy nodded. "I know. She had a hard morning. We went to her mom's place and— "

"*You* went to her mom's place?" Shelby stared at Katy with wide eyes.

"Uh-huh." Katy fiddled with the ribbon on her cap. "She—um, she asked me to spend the day with her, and I—well, I kinda thought she needed someone to be with her." Surely Shelby would see through that lame excuse! She hurried on. "But there was some man there—Hugo." Katy shuddered, remembering the uncomfortable feeling that crept over her when Hugo came into the house. "We left right away."

Shelby's jaw hung open. "Kathleen! That guy ... he might have ..." She flicked a glance right and left and then lowered her voice. "He doesn't keep his hands to himself, Kathleen. Don't *ever* go with Jewel again, okay? It's not ... safe."

Katy frowned. Since when did Shelby tell her what to do? Besides, she had no desire to return to Jewel's smelly house where Hugo lived.

"And you need to tell the office where you've been this morning."

Katy licked her dry lips. "They know I was gone?"

"Of course they do. The teachers take attendance and turn it in."

Katy nearly groaned. Why hadn't she remembered taking attendance when Jewel asked her to leave? The school handbook explained how the attendance secretary checked each teacher's report against her list of call-in absentees. Anyone who was missing but wasn't on her list got a follow-up call.

Shelby tipped forward, her brow puckering in concern. "They give you an unexcused absence if your parents don't call to say you'll be gone, and you can end up in detention. So you better go let them know where you were."

"A detention?" That meant staying after school. Katy swallowed. Dad would be very upset if she missed the bus and he had to drive clear in to Salina and get her.

Shelby's face twisted in sympathy. "Yeah, it could happen. But the principal is pretty nice. He might not give you a detention if you 'fess up. Especially since it's your first offense."

Katy sucked in a hopeful breath.

"But they *will* have called your dad by now."

Katy's breath whooshed out. She'd pushed Gramma Ruthie's reminder about choosing wisely right out of her mind when she'd taken off with Jewel. But now she'd be in trouble with the principal *and* with her dad. Her choices might mean having to withdraw from school if the deacons found out she'd left the campus without permission. Tears pricked her eyes, and she blinked several times to send them away.

She put her tray on the table, her appetite gone. "I better go talk to the principal now."

"Want me to come with you?"

Despite her worry, Katy smiled at Shelby's concern. "Thanks, but I need to do this alone."

"Okay. Good luck." Shelby squeezed Katy's shoulder and then headed for the lunch line.

Squaring her shoulders, Katy turned toward the office.

"I'm disappointed in you, Katy."

Katy swallowed the tears that gathered in her throat. It cut her to the core to hear the anger in his voice. She'd known by the look on his face when she climbed into the truck that the principal had managed to reach Dad through the telephone at the grocery store. How many other people in Schellberg knew what she'd done?

She clasped her hands in her lap and stared at her linked fingers. "I know. I'm sorry."

"Sorry isn't enough." Dad gripped the steering wheel as the truck bounced over a rut. "You could have come to all kinds of harm wandering away from the school and going to a strange neighborhood."

Katy, remembering Hugo, knew Dad was right. She gave him a pleading look. "But I couldn't let Jewel go alone, could I?" Her conscience pricked. She hadn't left with

Jewel to give the girl company; she'd gone out of curiosity. But Dad would never accept an excuse like that.

Dad sent her a quick frown before focusing on the road again. "She might not have gone at all if you'd said no to her request."

Katy nibbled her lip. She doubted that Jewel would have followed her lead, but she decided not to argue. She was in enough trouble.

Dad continued. "Or you could have gone in to the office and told them the girl was leaving. Then the principal would have taken care of it." He shook his head. "I expect you to use better judgment."

"I *am* sorry, Dad. I know it was wrong. I won't do it again — I promise!"

"No, you certainly won't do it again." Dad's lips formed a grim line.

Katy's heart pounded. What did Dad mean? Had the deacons already met and decided she should be withdrawn from school? Had one foolish decision ruined her chance to finish high school? "D-Dad?"

Dad's eyes flicked toward her. "What?"

His gruff tone didn't invite questions, but she couldn't hold it back. "Are you going to make me stop going to school?"

Dad didn't answer. They drove in silence until they reached the farm. Dad steered the truck to its spot beside the barn and turned off the ignition. He turned sideways in the seat and faced Katy.

"Katy, there will be a punishment for what you did today. I don't know yet what it will be. I don't know if it will be removing you from school. I need to think about it. If going to that school leads you to behave in ways that could be dangerous, then making you stay home would probably be best."

Katy's heart sank. Tears flooded her eyes. "But, Dad, I— "

He held up his hand. "I said I need to think about it, Katy. For now, go in the house and get supper started. We'll talk again before bedtime."

Katy scuttled out of the truck and ran to the house.

Chapter Seventeen

Katy considered preparing Dad's favorite meal—fried chicken, mashed potatoes and gravy, and corn with lots of butter. She meant it as an apology. But she feared he'd see it as a way of softening him up. So instead she made her own favorite—homemade macaroni and cheese. If Dad was going to tell her she couldn't return to school, she deserved a good meal beforehand.

But when Dad finished the milking and came in for dinner, she couldn't eat. Worry and guilt filled her stomach, making it impossible for her to swallow. She pushed the cheesy elbow noodles around on her plate instead of eating. Dad ate two hearty servings, but he didn't say a word while he ate, adding to Katy's tension. She could hardly wait to get the meal over so they could have their talk, Dad could give whatever punishment he'd chosen, and things could return to normal.

Whatever normal is.

Dad used a piece of bread to sop up the puddles of cheese on his plate and then wiped his mouth with a napkin. He rose. "Get the dishes done, Katy, and then homework."

Hope flickered in Katy's heart. If he expected her to do homework, surely that meant he wasn't going to pull her out of school!

"Gramma Ruthie and Grampa Ben will be over around eight. You need to have everything done by then so we can talk."

Although Dad's voice was calm and even, apprehension seized Katy. Why did Gramma Ruthie and Grampa Ben need to be involved? Wasn't it enough to have Dad disappointed in her? Gramma, especially, would be sad to learn Katy had behaved so foolishly after their talk about making good decisions.

Katy sniffed hard. "Yes, Dad." She rushed through kitchen clean up and escaped to her bedroom. She spread her homework across her desk, but she couldn't concentrate. So she pulled out her journal, opened it, and turned to a fresh page. Her pencil flew across the lines, pouring out her worry about what Dad would do, her unsettling time with Jewel, and her regret for leaving school that morning.

If I could do it over again, she wrote, *I'd tell Jewel no.* But then she wondered, would she? She'd been given a glimpse of another kind of life — a glimpse that helped her understand Jewel. After seeing Jewel's house and the man her mother called her "boyfriend," Katy now held sympathy for Jewel that overrode any feelings of dislike or frustration. Although she wished she had gained the insight a different way, she was glad she understood Jewel better. Her understanding would make dealing with Jewel easier. And now that Jewel knew she and Katy had something in common — a neglectful mother — maybe Jewel wouldn't be so critical of Katy.

She could hope, couldn't she?

"Katy!" Dad called from downstairs. "Come down, please."

Gramma and Grampa must have arrived. Katy drew in a big breath. Sending a quick glance toward the ceiling, she implored God, "Please don't let them be toooo mad . . ."

Katy entered the living room and found Dad sitting in his big overstuffed chair. He still wore a somber look, but the deep furrows in his forehead were smoothed out. The anger from earlier had apparently dissolved. She looked at Gramma and Grampa, who sat on the sofa. They appeared serious too. Katy missed their usual welcoming smiles.

"Here, Katy-girl." Gramma Ruthie patted the spot of sofa between her and Grampa Ben. "Come sit here and let's talk a little bit."

Katy clasped her hands in front of her and sat on the edge of the cushion. She glanced around at each of the adults and blew out a little breath. "Okay. I'm ready for my punishment."

Dad cleared his throat. He sat forward, resting his elbows on his knees and fitting his thumbnails together. Katy called the position his "thoughtful pose." She swallowed and waited for him to speak. But then he just sat staring at his thumbs without saying anything. Katy squirmed.

Gramma Ruthie finally patted Katy's knee. "Katy-girl, I think it's best if we let you talk first. Tell us why it wasn't a good idea to leave school today without asking."

Katy hunched her shoulders and pressed her sweaty palms flat on her knees. "Well, no one at the school knew where Jewel and I were, so that wasn't very smart. We got in a taxi with a stranger, and we went to a neighborhood where I ..." Unpleasant images filled Katy's head. She licked her lips. "Where I could have been hurt." Katy hung her head. "It was a stupid thing to do."

"Then why did you do it?" Gramma's soft voice held no recrimination.

Katy sent a quick glance at Dad before facing Gramma Ruthie. "Because Jewel asked me to. And Jewel ... I didn't want her to think I was weird. And I guess I wanted her to like me. To be my friend."

Dad's head shot up. "If she was really your friend, she wouldn't encourage you to break the school's rules."

Gramma clicked her tongue on her teeth. "Samuel ..."

Dad went back to examining his thumbs.

Gramma gave Katy's knee another pat. "Katy-girl, God put a good brain in your head. You know right from wrong, and you know your choices today put you in what could have been a dangerous situation. Not only did you put yourself in danger, but you worried your dad and your grampa and me."

Gramma's words, though kindly spoken, pierced Katy's heart. "I'm sorry, Gramma Ruthie. I didn't mean to worry anyone."

"I know that. I believe if you'd thought it all through, you would have stayed at school."

Gramma had more confidence in Katy than she had in herself. Katy kept silent.

"But now we aren't sure we can trust you. And that's an uncomfortable feeling."

Remorse sat heavily on Katy's shoulders. How much change could come from one unwise decision? She wanted to apologize, but her tongue felt thick and stiff. She couldn't speak.

"The thing is, Katy-girl, none of us expect you to grow up without making mistakes." Gramma slipped her arm around Katy's shoulders and tugged. Katy rested her head in the curve of Gramma's neck. "But we also expect you to learn from your mistakes and not make the same ones again and again. You know the school rules, and you know what you did today was against the school's rules, as well as foolish and reckless. What did you learn from it?"

Still nestled against Gramma's shoulder, Katy thought about the different sights and sounds of Jewel's neighborhood. She'd always known worldly people lived differently than those who resided in the little Mennonite community of Schellberg. But for the first time, she'd been exposed to ugly living. She felt as though she'd lost a little bit of her innocence while standing in Jewel's foul-smelling, filthy kitchen with Hugo looking her up and down. But how could she explain all of that to Gramma, Grampa, and Dad without giving them another reason to worry?

She chose her words carefully. "I learned that I need to follow my conscience instead of trying to fit in with people who might not care as much as we do about pleasing God. And that includes obeying the rules no matter what other people are doing." From the way Dad nodded, she knew she'd said the right thing. She sat up. "And from now on, that's what I'll do. I won't worry you again. I'll earn back your trust. I promise."

Grampa gave Katy's shoulders a squeeze. "I think we should pray for Katy. We sent her to that school where she's with kids who weren't raised like she was. She needs more of our support, I think."

"That's a good idea," Gramma agreed. "Samuel, you start."

Without hesitation, Dad closed his eyes and began to pray. "Dear Heavenly Father ..."

Katy scrunched her eyes closed and listened to Dad lift her to his Lord. Tears built up behind her closed eyelids and leaked out. His concern for her and his desire for her to be a godly woman came through in his voice. No punishment would have affected her as deeply as her father's heartfelt request for God to strengthen her and guide her on a righteous pathway.

Both Grampa and Gramma prayed too. By the time they were finished, Katy's cheeks were warm and moist from tears. She cleaned her face with her sleeve and stood. Dad rose too, his face tired and stern.

"Katy, as a consequence for your behavior today, you will spend two weeks doing extra chores. If I can't keep you busy here, then Aunt Rebecca can use you at the fabric shop after school."

Katy nearly groaned. She'd expected a punishment—she even believed she deserved one—but hours with Aunt Rebecca? Surely she didn't deserve that!

"Now go on up to bed."

Katy's shoulders drooped. "Yes, sir." She started for the stairs then turned back. She looked directly into her dad's eyes. "Dad, I really am sorry I worried you."

Dad nodded. "I know, Katy. Go on now."

She obediently went around the corner to the staircase. As her foot met the first riser, she heard Dad speak.

"Thanks, Mom and Dad, for being here. I didn't know what to say to her."

The frustration in his tone froze Katy in place. She knew she should go on up instead of listening, but she couldn't seem to make her feet move.

"You underestimate yourself, Son." Grampa spoke.

"No. I was so mad at her ..." A huge sigh sounded, and Katy envisioned Dad clenching his fists. "If it had been up to me, she'd be out of that school, away from those kids."

Katy held her breath.

"But that wouldn't be fair," Dad went on. "Not based on one mistake. I can't expect her to be perfect."

"No, you can't," Gramma's voice countered, "but you can expect her to learn from her mistakes. I think she learned from this one."

"I hope so ..."

Katy waited a few more seconds, but when no one else spoke, she started to climb the stairs. Then Dad's voice came again.

"Raising her would be so much easier if I had a wife to help me. A woman knows what to say to a girl. Katy needs a mother."

Grampa's chuckle reached Katy's ears. "We've been telling you that for the last five years."

"I know." Dad nearly growled the agreement. "But maybe for the first time I realize you're right. It's time for me to let Kate go for good and move on ... for both of our sakes."

Katy raced up the stairs.

Chapter Eighteen

The two weeks of Katy's punishment seemed to drag on forever. As Katy had feared, Dad couldn't keep her busy enough at the farm, so he dropped her off at Aunt Rebecca's shop every afternoon. And her time there became torture. Her aunt exhorted Katy on the virtues of following the guidelines of the fellowship and quoted Scripture after Scripture as a means of proving her points. Katy bit the end of her tongue to keep quiet and prayed for God to help her never again do something so awful that she earned another punishment like this one!

She counted down the days of her punishment by crossing them off on the calendar that hung in her bedroom. Finally October 21 — the last day — arrived. She nearly jumped up and down for happiness when she realized the two weeks had reached their end. Only one more day of listening to Aunt Rebecca's diatribes! She tapped the numbered square on the calendar, savoring the word *diatribe.* She'd encountered it in her English book a few days ago and decided it was a perfect word for Aunt Rebecca's endless criticism. She'd even taken to chanting it inside her head—*Diatribe, diatribe, diatribe*—to drown out her aunt's scolding voice.

"One more day ... I can handle one more day," she whispered to encourage herself. But maybe she wouldn't have to go. If she rounded up all the dirty laundry, Dad might let her come home and wash clothes instead of taking her to Aunt Rebecca's shop. She dressed quickly and dashed out of her room in search of dirty clothes.

When Dad came in from milking, he almost tripped over the mountain of dresses, pants, shirts, and towels Katy had dumped beside the back door. He pointed. "What's all this?"

"Laundry." Katy flipped the eggs in the skillet. "I thought I'd get it done after school today. If that's okay with you."

A lopsided smile formed on Dad's face, but then he cleared his throat and the smile disappeared. "I suppose. But don't leave it here. It'll be in my way."

"Yes, sir!"

While they were eating, Dad suddenly lowered his eyebrows and sighed. "I wish there was a way to get you to school earlier on Wednesday."

Katy paused in taking a bite of toast. "Why?"

"That Bible study Reverend Nuss mentioned ... I think it would be good for you to meet with other students who are Christians."

Katy nodded. "I'd like that. But the bus doesn't get there in time."

"I know." Dad forked up a bite of eggs and chewed slowly. "Maybe Grampa Ben would take you in early on Wednesdays ... I'll ask him."

Katy dropped her toast and flew around the table to hug her dad's neck. "Thank you, Dad!"

"You're welcome." He patted her arm and then pointed to her plate. "Now finish eating so we can get you to the bus on time."

Katy could hardly wait to tell Shelby she might be able to start attending the Bible study group. She met up with Shelby in the hall on the way to their first class, but before she could say anything, Shelby grabbed her arm and pulled her close.

"Kathleen, can you keep a secret?"

Katy nodded.

Shelby steered her from the middle of the milling throng to the edge of the hall. They inched their way toward class. "Jewel's sixteenth birthday is two weeks away. My family's planning a surprise party on November six, and you're invited."

Katy stared in amazement. Ever since Shelby had telephoned her dad out of concern for Jewel, Jewel had alternately ignored and sniped at Shelby. There were times Katy wondered how Shelby maintained her sanity, having Jewel living under her roof. "That's really nice of you."

"Well, a girl only turns sixteen once, and we want it to be special. Especially since she won't be able to spend her birthday with her mom."

Despite Jewel's unpleasant behavior, sympathy still welled when Katy thought about how Jewel's mother chose to let Hugo stay in her house rather than have Jewel move home again. "I'll ask my dad if I can come. Your dad will probably have to call him, though." Even though her punishment was ending, Katy hadn't yet earned back her dad's trust. That would take more than two weeks.

"I'll have him do that. But remember, Kathleen — don't mention it to Jewel!"

Shelby and Katy joined Cora, Bridget, and Trisha at lunch. Shelby filled them in on the plans for Jewel's party.

Cora squealed. "Oooh! Fun! Will it be an overnighter?"

"Will you invite boys?" Bridget asked. "If it's Jewel's party, she'll expect to have boys there."

Katy almost giggled. Bridget's question sounded like something Annika would ask. Annika probably wouldn't like it if Katy told her she and Bridget had something in common. Annika still resisted any mention of high school and the people Katy spent time with each school day.

"We're inviting the youth kids from church," Shelby said, "girls and boys both. So there'll be boys."

"Not the boys Jewel would want." Bridget raised one eyebrow. "Are you sure this party is for Jewel, or is it for your family?"

Katy glanced across the lunchroom and spotted Jewel sitting with a group of kids Cora had tagged "the skaters." One of the boys draped his arm around Jewel's neck and whispered something in her ear. She laughed and pushed him away, but her smile never wavered. Katy wondered if Bridget was right. Jewel would probably rather have her friends at her party than Shelby's friends.

Shelby puckered her lips for a moment, then she shook her head. "The party is for Jewel — to help her understand that she's a part of our family now. If everyone who comes includes her and makes her feel welcome, maybe she'll finally start to settle in with us. You know, really become part of the family."

"I hope it works," Bridget said, but her tone didn't sound very hopeful.

"It will." Shelby picked up a french fry and used it to

point at each of the girls in turn. "And all of you will help. You'll all be there with presents and smiles and complete acceptance no matter how awful she acts. And we all know she can act pretty awful."

A mumble of agreement went around the circle of girls. Katy leaned forward. "I've never bought a gift for a ..." Would the girls be offended? "A worldly person. I don't think Jewel would like any of the things I'd buy for one of my friends in Schellberg. What should I get?"

Cora waved her hands. "Oh, oh, Kathleen! If Jewel was Mennonite, what would you get her?" Her eyes sparkled with curiosity.

Katy raised one shoulder. "Well, sixteen's a big year. A girl is finished with school by then ... usually ... and she's old enough to start attending the community parties with the other unmarried people. Which means she can start accepting the attention of a young man. So on her sixteenth birthday, people get her things for her hope chest."

"Hope chest?" Trisha pressed her fingertips to her bodice and looked at her front. "You mean she starts hoping her chest gets bigger?"

Bridget and Cora squealed with laughter. Shelby smacked Trisha's wrist. "Be serious."

"I *am* serious," Trisha said, her eyes wide. "I don't think they're ever going to show up!"

Katy bit her lower lip and looked away. Talking about a person's *attributes* wasn't polite conversation.

Shelby whacked Trisha again, but she laughed. "I mean it. Knock it off."

Trisha sighed. "Okay, okay. Sorry, Kathleen. So what's a hope chest, anyway?"

Katy turned back. The girls did appear interested, so she explained, "In our community, when a girl becomes a teenager, she starts learning to keep house and to be a good wife and mother. She usually has a trunk or chest, called a hope chest, where she keeps things she'll use when she moves into her own home — linens, pretty dishes, quilts ... things like that." Katy's favorite items in her hope chest were lovely embroidered table runners and dresser scarves, hand-stitched by Gramma Ruthie.

Cora's mouth hung open. "That's totally cool! I want a hope chest!"

Trisha laughed. "You aren't Mennonite."

"Okay, so I wanna be Mennonite!"

Trisha laughed again.

Katy said, "I'm pretty sure anybody can have a hope chest. You don't have to be Mennonite."

"Sweet." Cora flashed a smile around the table. "I'm gonna ask my mom for a hope chest for my sixteenth."

"Good," Shelby said, shaking her head and grinning at Katy, "but we still haven't answered Kathleen's question about what to get Jewel. Let's help her out, guys."

Immediately, the girls began tossing ideas at Katy: jewelry, a beaded cami, funky socks, hair ornaments, CDs ... Katy's head began to spin. Dad wouldn't let her buy any of those things! She held up both hands to bring an end to the flood of suggestions.

"I'll come up with something. Thanks."

The remainder of the day, thoughts of Jewel's upcoming party held Katy's attention. Would Dad let her go? What should she bring for a gift? Shelby wanted the party to be a way to let Jewel know she had friends and a place of belonging. Even if Dad said she couldn't attend the party, Katy wanted to give Jewel a special gift.

On the bus, Katy finally settled on an idea, but she'd need help from Aunt Rebecca. She pressed her forehead to the bus window. She'd finally been given freedom from going to Aunt Rebecca's shop every day. Did she really want to go there again? Then she thought about Jewel's face when she'd said, "How would you feel if your mother chose something like *him* over you?" And she knew she had to ask Dad for one more day with Aunt Rebecca.

Dad's eyebrows shot up when Katy climbed into the truck and immediately asked if he would take her to Aunt Rebecca's. "I thought you were going to do laundry."

"I can still do it after supper. Some of that stuff could wait until Saturday."

He sat with his hand on the gearshift. "What do you need at Aunt Rebecca's?"

Katy sucked in a big breath. She hoped Dad wouldn't tell her no. "Remember Jewel from school?" Dad frowned. Katy hurried on. "She turns sixteen in two more weeks. I want to make something for her — something special. And I need Aunt Rebecca to help me."

"You're doing this for Jewel?" He sounded worried. And confused.

"Yes. I'm not going to get into any trouble. I just want to give her a gift that tells her ... well, that she's special." Katy gave Dad her best imploring look. "She's had a rough life, Dad. And I just think she needs somebody to be extra nice to her. Besides, didn't Jesus teach that whatever we do for the least of these, we also do for Him?"

For a long time Dad sat and looked into Katy's face,

his expression unreadable. Finally he nodded. "All right, Katy." He put the truck into gear and turned it around. "I'll pick you up from Rebecca's shop after I've finished the milking."

"Thanks, Dad." Katy settled back in the seat and smiled. Maybe Dad was starting to trust her again ... at least a little bit. Dad pulled up outside Aunt Rebecca's shop and Katy hopped out. "I'll see you later!" She skipped across the wooden walkway and entered the shop. "Hi, Aunt Rebecca."

"Katy ..." Aunt Rebecca paused in cutting off a length of blue floral fabric. "I didn't know if you were coming in today. I didn't set aside any work for you."

Katy stood on the opposite side of the tall cutting table and rested her fingers on its edge. "I'm not here to work. I came to talk to you about a special project. I want to make a friendship quilt—not a full-sized one, but one that could hang on a wall. Can you help me figure out how much fabric I need and help me choose some pretty patterns?"

Aunt Rebecca smoothed her ribbons behind her shoulders. "Why certainly, Katy. Do you have a particular color scheme in mind?" She headed toward the shelves that held upright bolts of cloth.

Katy trailed behind, tapping her chin with her finger. "I think something bold—bright and happy."

Aunt Rebecca stopped and pulled out a bolt of sapphire blue fabric with deeper blue squiggles. The pattern reminded Katy of streamers sailing through the air. "Like this?"

Katy clapped her hands together. "Yes! That's perfect! It's cheerful, and it's jewel-toned!" She giggled even though she knew Aunt Rebecca wouldn't understand that she'd just made a little joke. "I'll use the blue, and that yellow, this pink . . . and that green." She slipped the bolts from the shelves and stacked them in Aunt Rebecca's arms. "Will that be enough?"

"You'll need a light color to form the center of the block where you'll do the writing." Aunt Rebecca bobbed her head toward another shelf. "I suggest white rather than ivory cotton. With these bright colors, ivory will look dirty."

Katy retrieved a bolt of white cotton and followed Aunt Rebecca to the cutting table.

"How many blocks will your quilt have?"

Katy counted off the girls by flipping her fingers upward—Shelby, Trisha, Cora, Bridget, Jewel, and herself. "Six."

Aunt Rebecca frowned at the stack. "Well, then I would suggest either putting one of these fabrics back and making two blocks out of each remaining fabric, or selecting two more colors and making one block of each fabric."

Katy looked over at the shelf. After a moment's thought, she chose orange and purple fabrics. She couldn't stop smiling. This quilt would be as bold as the girl who would own it!

Aunt Rebecca punched several numbers into the little calculator that sat on the corner of the table and figured out how much of each fabric Katy would need. Then she sketched a pattern on a piece of graph paper and wrote the instructions for cutting the fabric into pieces to form the blocks. Less than an hour after entering the shop, Katy had everything she needed to begin creating Jewel's friendship quilt.

"Thanks so much, Aunt Rebecca," Katy said. Her time

with her aunt this afternoon had been pleasant, and she coupled her thanks with a big smile.

"You're welcome. Now,"—she punched in a few more numbers on her calculator—"that all adds up to forty-two dollars and sixty cents, including tax."

Katy's smile faded. She'd become so used to working to earn fabric for dresses, she'd forgotten about paying the bill. "I—I don't have any money with me."

Aunt Rebecca's brows pulled down. "Well, Katy, I know I usually pay you for your work, but I can't pay for the past two weeks. That was a part of your punishment."

Katy didn't need the reminder. She nodded miserably.

Her aunt fingered the edge of the pink fabric. "I tell you what ... I'll put this on a tab, and we'll let you 'pay it off' by working the next few Saturdays. Is that all right?"

"Oh, thank you!"

The little bell above the door jingled. Katy turned to see Annika and her sister Taryn enter the shop. Taryn said, "Hello, Mrs. Lambright. We came to choose some fabric to make Dad a couple of shirts."

"I'll be glad to help you, girls," Aunt Rebecca said. "Let me package up Katy's friendship quilt fabrics, and then I'll be right with you."

Annika's lips tipped up in a knowing smile. "A friendship quilt?"

Katy's heart turned a somersault in her chest.

Chapter Nineteen

An idea — a bold idea — filled Katy's mind. Depending on how it was accepted, her friendship with Annika would either be strengthened or shattered, but she had to ask.

"Aunt Rebecca, can Annika and I go in the back room to talk for a minute?"

Aunt Rebecca's brows lowered briefly, but she nodded. Katy grabbed Annika's hand and tugged her through the curtained doorway that led to the workroom. She fluffed the curtain back in place over the door opening and spun to face Annika.

"I have a really big favor to ask you."

Annika folded her arms over her chest. "You've got a lot of nerve, asking me for a favor when you've practically ignored me since Caleb's party. But then — " Her expression turned smug — "I guess with your punishment, you really *couldn't* spend time with me, could you?"

Katy stifled a sigh. In Schellberg, everyone knew everybody else's business. Of course Annika would be aware of the trouble Katy had gotten into at school. She licked her lips. "No, I couldn't. But ... honestly, Annika, you haven't exactly been seeking me out, either. Not since I started school. And ... I miss you."

Annika fingered the ribbons on her cap and looked to the side. She shrugged slowly. "Well ... I guess I've missed you too ... sort of."

The half-hearted reply didn't exactly fill Katy with confidence, but she pressed onward anyway, hoping for the best. "I'd like to spend time together again. And I could really use your help with something."

Annika scowled. "What?"

Katy drew in a deep breath. "Two weeks from now, one of the girls from school—her name is Jewel—will turn sixteen."

Annika took a step backward. "Is that the same Jewel who ...?"

Katy nodded so hard the ribbons on her cap bounced. She grabbed them and tossed them over her shoulder. "She's the one. Annika, this girl ... her life has been one big mess. I don't think anyone, ever—not even her own mother—has treated her like she mattered."

Annika tipped her head to the side. "What does that have to do with me?"

"Well, remember when you told me I wasn't telling people about God at my school?" Katy waited for Annika's nod before proceeding. "I got to thinking about that, and I realized that I had a chance to make a difference. To maybe be a ... I don't know, glimpse of Jesus ... to some of the kids there. And Jewel *really* needs it."

Annika moved closer to Katy. "But what does that have to do with *me*?" Her tone held a hint of impatience.

"That fabric I just bought is so I can make Jewel a

friendship quilt for her birthday. But I only have two weeks, and that isn't very much time. Would ... would you help me?" Katy held her breath.

For several seconds Annika stood and stared at Katy with her face crunched into a frown. Finally she shook her head. "I don't know this girl at all ..."

"I know, but you do know me, and I'll tell her how you helped." Katy skipped forward and caught Annika's hands. "Think about it. If a girl she doesn't even know is willing to help make her birthday special, don't you think Jewel will start to realize that *she* is special and worthy of kindness? You could make a real difference in her life, Annika. Will you help me?"

Annika looked at the ceiling for a moment. Then she looked into Katy's face. "I still think you're weird for doing all of this for some girl who got you into trouble, but ... okay. I'll help you."

Katy squealed and hugged Annika. "Thank you! I'll give you the backing piece so you can embroider a Bible verse on it. You do such a neat job with embroidering letters."

A pleased grin twitched on Annika's lips. "What verse do you want?"

"Proverbs seventeen, verse seventeen: 'A friend loveth at—' "

" '—All times,' " Annika finished in a whisper. Her chin began to quiver.

Concern rose in Katy's chest. "Annika, what's wrong?"

"Oh, Katy ..." Annika gulped. "I haven't loved *you* at all times." She choked out a sob. "I've been jealous and mean. I've been a terrible friend. I'm sorry."

Katy grabbed Annika in another hug. "It's okay. I know

my going to school has been hard on you. I know I've changed ... and that made our friendship change. But you're still my best friend. You always will be."

The girls hugged long and hard. Then Annika pulled back and sniffled. She offered a wobbly smile. "Well, give me that fabric and some floss so I can get busy on Jewel's verse."

Katy smoothed the finished friendship quilt across the foot of her bed and smiled at it. She nudged Annika with her elbow. "It looks good, doesn't it?"

Annika ran her finger over Shelby's name, which was embroidered in bright blue thread in the center of a white square. The thread seemed to glow, offset by the vivid blue fabric that formed a frame around the white center. "It does. I'm glad we got it done in time." She wiggled her fingers at Katy. "I've got calluses from the needle!"

Katy laughed. "But we did it." Every evening, the girls had met in Katy's bedroom to work on the quilt. The quilt had helped mend her and Annika's friendship in addition to creating a beautiful gift. The nine-inch blocks, set three-by-two, had a rainbow effect. Katy hoped Jewel would appreciate all of the time and effort that had gone into creating the quilt. "And now I better get it packaged." She pulled a gift bag from under her bed. "Look what Dad let me get to wrap it in."

Annika sucked in a startled breath. "Oh, Katy, it's perfect!" The gift bag boasted a large, arching rainbow studded with tiny rhinestones. "The bag is a gift all by itself. I hope she doesn't throw it away."

"Me too! Help me fold the quilt and get the tissue around it, would you?"

The girls giggled as they folded the quilt into a neat square, bundled it with sheets of crinkly white tissue paper, and stuffed it into the bag.

Annika fluffed the tissue sticking out of the bag's top. "What time is the party?"

"Seven o'clock tomorrow evening. But I'm going to Shelby's after school to help set up for it." Katy hunched her shoulders. "Jewel is clueless—has no idea they're planning a party. Mr. and Mrs. Nuss are going to take her out to supper, and while they're out Shelby, me, and some of the youth kids will decorate the house. Then when Jewel comes back, we'll all be hiding, and we'll jump out and yell 'surprise!' "

Annika grinned. "I like that idea! You can do it for me on my sixteenth."

Katy laughed. "But if you know we're going to do it, it won't be a surprise."

"I can *act* surprised." Annika made a google-eyed, open-mouthed look with her widespread hands beside her face. Then she flicked Katy's shoulder with her fingers. "Just make sure Caleb is there, and that'll be more than enough party for me."

Katy rolled her eyes. Annika and her endless infatuation with Caleb ... Well, Annika could have him! Katy did her best to avoid the milking barn when Caleb was around. He was still the most annoying person she knew—and her circle of acquaintance had grown plenty since she started high school.

"Yeah, well, your sixteenth isn't until next March, so we'll worry about it then. For now, I'll see if Dad will let me drive you home." Her chest puffed with pride as she remembered the driving lessons she'd taken from Grampa

Ben in the past two weeks. Dad said it was time she learned so she could drive herself to town if need be. She hadn't driven alone yet, but Annika's house was so close, surely Dad would agree.

"Absolutely not." Dad frowned at Katy and set his newspaper aside. "You aren't ready for that."

Oh, I'm ready; you're not ready to let me. Katy exchanged a wry grin with Annika.

Dad rose from his chair. "I'll drive Annika home. Go get in the truck, girls."

✣

At lunch the following day, Katy joined Shelby, Trisha, Cora, and Bridget, as had become customary over the weeks of school. Today the girls were especially giggly, excited about the party that evening. Although Katy managed to keep herself controlled, she couldn't stop a smile from growing on her face when Jewel plunked her tray down across from her. Would Jewel lose her disinterested expression tonight when everyone jumped out and surprised her? But her smile faded when Jewel sent Shelby a disgusted look.

"Tell me again ... *why* do I have to go to dinner with your parents?"

Shelby put her fork down. "Jewel, it's tradition in our family. On your birthday, you get to choose any restaurant in town, and Mom and Dad take you for a special dinner."

Jewel rolled her eyes. "As if I want to spend my birthday night with Mr. and Mrs. Preacher. What if I don't want to go?"

Cora burst out, "You *want* to go!"

Bridget slammed Cora's shoulder with the heel of her hand, nearly knocking Cora out of her chair.

Jewel narrowed her eyes and glared at Cora. "Why do I *want* to go?"

Cora sent a frantic look around the table. "Well . . . because . . . you'll hurt their feelings if you don't."

Jewel snorted. "As I said . . . why?"

Shelby leaned her elbows on the table. "Listen, Jewel, it's a big deal to Mom and Dad to do something special for birthdays."

"I'd rather do my own thing," Jewel said.

Katy believed it — Jewel's mom had apparently set that example for her. But Jewel now had a choice to make — graciously accept the offer from Shelby's parents or reject it. She could be like her mom, satisfying herself, or she could please the Nusses. Suddenly it became very important to Katy that Jewel do the opposite of what her mother would do.

"It's just one dinner," Katy said, putting her hand on Jewel's wrist. "And it means a lot to them. Can't you suffer through one dinner? Sometimes doing something to make somebody else happy, even if we don't want to, gives us happiness in the end. Try it, Jewel."

Jewel stared at Katy for a long time. Then she released another little snort. "Oh, whatever." A conniving smile curled her lips. "But if it's my choice of places, they might regret it. I've been wanting to go that fancy-shmancy Japanese restaurant out by the movie theater where they chop up the food and stuff right by your table. Will they take me there if I ask?"

Shelby nearly wilted. Relief showed in her eyes. "They'll take you anywhere in town."

Jewel stabbed her fork into the green beans on her

plate. "Great." She jammed the beans into her mouth and spoke around them. "If I gotta hang out with Mr. and Mrs. Preacher, might as well milk it . . ."

Shelby sent Katy a grateful look, and Katy winked in reply. After school, Katy trailed Shelby and Jewel to Mrs. Nuss's car. Jewel poked her thumb at Katy.

"Why's she comin' with us?"

Shelby and her mom exchanged a quick glance, and Mrs. Nuss said, "Shelby and Kathleen have a project to complete this evening." She took the large paper grocery sack from Katy that disguised Jewel's gift bag and put it in the trunk. "Is that everything, Kathleen?"

"Yes, ma'am." Katy swallowed a snicker as she climbed into the backseat with Shelby. When they reached the Nuss house, Jewel headed downstairs to watch television, and Katy and Shelby huddled in the bedroom, sorting through the decorations Mrs. Nuss had purchased. Katy glanced at the clock every few minutes. Time crept so slowly it seemed to stand still.

Finally five o'clock arrived, and Shelby's dad returned from the church. A few minutes later, Shelby's parents left with Jewel, who scuffed out the door wearing her usual bored face. Katy couldn't wait to see that face erased! The moment the car left the driveway, Katy and Shelby flew into action. They strung colored streamers from the ceiling light to the outer walls in the living room, creating a crinkling canopy of color. Katy blew up balloons until she was out of breath, and Shelby taped a huge banner proclaiming, "Happy 16th birthday, Jewel!" on the wall facing the front door.

Shelby carried up a huge cake that her mother had hidden in the basement laundry room — "Jewel never goes in there," Shelby proclaimed — and set out plates, cups, and plastic forks. Katy decorated a table to hold Jewel's gifts and placed her rainbow gift bag right in the middle. Her heart pounded as she considered Jewel's reaction to the gift. *Oh, please let her like it!* So much work had gone into the quilt. If Jewel acted bored or indifferent, Katy didn't know how she'd handle it.

Other kids began arriving around six, and the excitement level raised to a near fever pitch. Although Katy hadn't been around Shelby's youth group before, they treated her as if she'd always been a part of the gang.

At six forty-five, Shelby instructed everyone to find hiding places. Some kids crouched behind the couch and chairs in the living room; others zipped around the corner into the kitchen or plastered themselves against the hallway wall. Shelby turned out all the lights in the house. Someone — one of the boys, Katy was sure — let out an evil *bwa-ha-ha* laugh, and several girls squealed.

"Shh!" Shelby cautioned.

Muted giggles floated around the shadowy room.

Katy stationed herself at the window and peeked out from a slit in the curtains. The muscles in her legs twitched and her heart thudded in her chest. Were all surprise parties this exciting? She could hardly wait to see the look on Jewel's face! At five 'til seven, a car pulled into the driveway, and Katy hissed, "They're here!"

Shelby dashed out of her hiding spot and joined Katy. But then she frowned. "That's not Dad's car."

The girls watched as a woman stepped out of the vehicle and then stood in the driveway, looking toward the house. The porch light illuminated her face. Shelby gasped.

"Who is it?" Katy whispered.

"That's Jewel's mom!"

Chapter Twenty

"What should we do?" Shelby whispered.

Katy grabbed the doorknob. "Let her in."

"But—but— "

"Shelby, what better surprise than *her own mother* being at her party? You know Jewel will want her here." Katy swallowed a lump of jealousy. She'd give anything to have her own mother walk into her life. But that couldn't happen.

"But what if her boyfriend shows up too?"

Katy peeked out again. Jewel's mother still stood beside the car, looking toward the house with her hands deep in the pockets of her jacket. "There's nobody with her. She just wants to see her daughter on her birthday. We can't leave her out there." Something else struck Katy. "And we need to have her move her car or she'll ruin the surprise!"

Shelby nudged Katy out of the way and dashed out the door. Katy pressed her nose to the window and watched Shelby trot to Jewel's mother. Her arms flew out as she talked, and then Jewel's mother got into her car. She backed out of the driveway and disappeared around the corner. Shelby paced on the lawn, looking up and down the street.

A moment later, she gestured — a frantic waving of her hand — and Jewel's mom jogged onto the lawn. Together, the two came into the house.

"Kathleen," Shelby said as she closed the door, "this is Mrs. Hamilton."

"*Ms.* Hamilton," the woman corrected. Her voice held a hard undercurrent that reminded Katy of Jewel. "But you can call me Becky."

"It's nice to meet you," Katy said, but she couldn't bring herself to call the woman by her first name. She pointed toward the kitchen where two kids peeked out in curiosity. "Do you want to hide in there?"

Mrs. Hamilton raised her eyebrows.

Shelby said, "We're all planning to jump out and surprise Jewel when she gets back."

"All?" The woman sounded skeptical.

Several heads peeked out of hiding places. Kids waggled their fingers in shy hellos. Jewel's mother looked around, her eyebrows high.

Katy said, "Jewel will be really happy to see you."

"Yeah. Yeah, I hope so . . ."

Shelby pointed at her wristwatch and shot Katy a frantic look. Katy stepped forward. "Go ahead and go into the kitchen, Mrs. — Ms. Hamilton. We'll let you know when Jewel gets here."

Ms. Hamilton glanced around at the decorations again and whistled through her teeth as she walked toward the kitchen. Just as she stepped around the corner, Katy heard another car. She whirled and peeked out. "*Now* they're here!"

Shelby grabbed Katy's hand and together they dashed behind the nearest chair. Katy held her breath, listening to the soft mumble of voices carrying from outside. The doorknob turned, and when the door opened Shelby yelped out, "Surprise!"

On cue, the other kids leaped from their hiding places, hollering, "Surprise! Surprise!"

Jewel stumbled backward, her mouth wide open. Katy clapped and called, "Surprise, Jewel! Happy birthday!"

Mr. Nuss flipped on the lights, and everyone swarmed Jewel, pulling her into the center of the room. Her gaze bounced from the kids to the streamers to the banner. Her mouth stayed open, as if she couldn't believe what she was seeing. Katy laughed and looked around the sea of smiling, happy faces. But one face was missing. Had Jewel's mother sneaked out the back door?

She separated herself from the talking, laughing group and hurried to the kitchen. Jewel's mother stood in the far corner, leaning against the counter. Her arms were wrapped across her middle, and she looked as uncomfortable as Katy had felt her first day of school.

Katy edged up beside her. "Ms. Hamilton, aren't you going to come tell Jewel happy birthday?"

The woman pushed her hair behind her ear and waved her hand toward the living room. "That table of presents out there ..." She raised her chin, her expression defensive. "I didn't bring a gift."

Katy thought about her own mother, and she knew exactly what to say. "Having you here will be present enough for Jewel. Please come out."

Ms. Hamilton ran her hands through her hair again then tugged her jacket down over the waistband of her jeans. She nodded. "All right." Katy led her around the corner. Jewel stood in the center of the kids with her back to Katy. Katy called, "Jewel?"

Jewel turned. "What?" And then her eyes bugged. "Mom?"

The group of kids fell silent.

Ms. Hamilton took one shuffling step forward. "Happy birthday, Jewel."

Jewel's lips flew into a smile, but then she ran her hand over her mouth, resuming her normal, I-don't-care face. But she bobbed her head in a greeting. "G-good to see you. Did ..." Her gaze jerked around the room. "Did Hugo come with you?"

Jewel's mother hung her head for a moment. "He's ... at home."

Jewel nodded, and something in her eyes made Katy's heart ache. Jewel's mother was here, at her party, but she hadn't stepped fully back into Jewel's life. The silence in the room lengthened, becoming uncomfortable. Somebody needed to say something. Katy poked Shelby, who jumped and let out a little squeak. Someone tittered, and then two more people laughed, and some of the tension drained from the room.

Mr. Nuss threw his arm around Jewel's shoulders. "What do you want to do first—eat cake or open presents?"

"Cake! Cake!" the boys chanted.

But Jewel held her stomach with both hands. "I can't eat cake yet. I'm too full. So let's do presents."

The boys moaned, elbowing each other. Katy rolled her eyes. Boys! Were they always hungry? One of them clutched his stomach and collapsed onto the floor in a fake faint. The others laughed, and Katy had to cover her mouth to hold back her own giggles.

Jewel sat on the sofa, and Mrs. Nuss insisted Ms. Hamilton sit beside her. Kids perched everywhere—on the furniture, on the floor, wherever they could find a spot. Shelby and Katy took turns carrying gifts to Jewel. She opened them carefully, folding the wrapping paper and making a neat stack beside the couch. She passed the gifts around so everyone could admire them.

Katy's heart nearly pounded out of her chest when she handed Jewel the rainbow gift bag containing the quilt. As soon as Jewel took it, Katy clasped her hands together and scuttled back to the gift table. Jewel clicked her red-painted fingernail on the rhinestones. "Cool bag—this is epic." She checked the little name tag. "This came from Kathleen? No way!"

"Way," Katy said automatically, imitating kids she'd heard at school. A laugh blasted from the group, but Katy ignored it. She watched Jewel reach into the bag and tug out the tissue-wrapped bundle. Jewel unwrapped it slowly. The quilt fell open across her knees in an explosion of colors. Several girls released little "ohs" and sat forward to get a better look. Jewel touched each square that held a name, her brows low. Then she shot a puzzled look at Katy. "Did you make this?"

Katy nodded. "It—it's a friendship quilt. Since you, Shelby, Trisha, Cora, and Bridget spend so much time together at school, I put all of your names on the front. Mine too." Her ears heated, and she scurried forward to flip the quilt onto its back. The verse from Proverbs filled the center in Annika's neat, calligraphic script. "One of my friends from Schellberg embroidered the verse. But we left lots of space, and I brought a fabric pen with me so everyone here can sign the back, if you want them to."

Jewel stared at the quilt. "This is ... real nice, Kathleen. Thanks." There was little enthusiasm in her tone, but Katy knew Jewel was good at hiding her feelings. So Katy wasn't offended.

Jewel's mother smiled up at Katy. "Yes, it's very nice. You're a talented girl."

Katy's ears burned even hotter. "Thank you."

Jewel handed the quilt to Katy. "Yeah, if people wanna sign it, that's fine." She looked straight into Katy's face. She didn't smile, but the bored look was gone. "It's real cool, Kathleen. Thanks."

Katy smiled and nodded.

"Get to the rest of the presents," one of the boys hollered, "so we can eat cake!"

Jewel shook her head and rolled her eyes. But then she laughed and reached for the next gift.

The remainder of the evening passed quickly, and at ten o'clock kids left for their own homes. Katy retrieved her backpack from Shelby's bedroom so Mr. Nuss could drive her home. When she entered the living room, Jewel stepped into her pathway. Jewel stood with her weight on one hip — an insolent pose. Katy hugged her backpack, uncertain what to expect.

"Cora told me that quilt you made is supposed to be for my hope chest." A funny grin twitched at the corner of Jewel's mouth. "I don't have one of those."

Katy licked her lips. "You don't have to put it in a chest. You can hang it on the wall or drape it over a chair."

"Oh, I know. I'm just kidding." Jewel sighed, glancing toward the kitchen. Her mother leaned on the doorjamb, sipping a cup of coffee. "I don't have a hope chest, and I don't have much hope of my mom ever ..." She swallowed and looked at Katy again. "But hey—at least she was here, right? That's something."

Katy nodded eagerly. "It's a lot." More than I'll ever have ... She touched Jewel's shoulder. "Happy birthday."

"Yeah. It was ... happy."

Mr. Nuss bustled forward. "You're ready, Kathleen? Good—I told your dad I'd have you home by ten thirty, so we'd better get moving."

As Katy left, she glanced over her shoulder in time to see Jewel saunter to her mother's side. Ms. Hamilton reached out and tucked Jewel's hair behind her ear. Jealousy stabbed through Katy's chest as she hurried after Mr. Nuss.

✣

Sunday before service, Annika panted to Katy's side as she hung her sweater on a peg in the women's cloakroom. "Did she like it?"

Katy spun and hugged Annika. "She *loved* it."

"What did she say?"

Katy drew in a deep breath. Annika didn't know Jewel the way Katy did, and she didn't want Annika to feel the gift had been a flop. "It's not so much what she said, but how she looked when she opened it. Jewel's not very good at expressing herself, but I know she loved it."

Annika grinned. "Good. Wanna sit with me?"

"Sure!" They linked arms and entered the meeting room together. Katy waggled her fingers at Gramma Ruthie, who sat in one of the benches toward the front. Gramma waved back and then turned to visit with a lady on her right. Katy frowned in curiosity. She'd never seen that woman in Schellberg before. She started to ask Annika if she knew who the woman was, but Deacon Knepp stepped to the front of the worship hall and opened his Bible, signaling the start of service.

When the service was over, Katy and Annika wandered out into the yard. November had arrived, and the trees were absent of leaves, but the day was pleasant and comfortable. People lingered, enjoying the sunshine and soft breeze. Annika tugged Katy to a small circle of young people that included Caleb. *Of course . . .*

Caleb gave Katy a smirk. "Hey, Katydid, are you still under lock and key, or has your dad let you loose?"

The other boys snickered softly, and Katy's ears went hot. "Why do you need to know?"

"There's a corn shucking at the Stenzel place this coming Friday. Wondered if you'd be there. But maybe you're not allowed to go to parties again just yet . . ."

Katy flicked a glance at Annika. She'd finally regained her friendship with Annika — would Caleb mess things up again?

To her surprise, Annika scowled at Caleb and propped her fist on her hip. "Not that it's *your* business, Caleb Penner, but Katy went to a party last night. *In Salina.* So if she wants to go to Andy Stenzel's party she can. And if she doesn't want to, she won't. Either way, it has nothing to do with *you.*" She stuck her nose in the air and flounced away, dragging Katy with her.

Well away from the group, Katy released a giggle. "Annika! What was that all about?"

Annika sniffed. "Oh, that Caleb. He's just too full of himself sometimes. It aggravates me." She glanced over her shoulder at Caleb and the other boys. Caleb gawked across the grass at them. Annika gave a satisfied grin. "And I'm pretty sure he talks to you to try to make me jealous." She flipped her head, making her ribbons dance. "Well, it isn't going to work."

Katy laughed out loud.

"Katy-girl?" Dad called from the edge of the church-yard. "Dinner time. Let's go."

"Okay, Dad!"

Annika grabbed her arm. "See if you can walk over this afternoon. This nice weather won't last. While it's so pretty, we should go down by the creek and sit and talk."

"I'll ask," Katy promised.

"Katy!" Dad sounded impatient.

"Coming!" Katy raced to Dad's side. "Where are we going for dinner today? Gramma Ruthie's?"

Dad scratched his chin. "Yes. And ..."

Apprehension made Katy's scalp tingle. "And?"

Dad put his hand on Katy's shoulder. "We won't be the only ones there."

On most Sundays, Gramma Ruthie invited several people to dinner. Katy couldn't understand why Dad looked so serious. "Who else is coming?"

"Gramma invited a ... cousin's friend. From Meade County."

Katy remembered the lady sitting with Gramma in service. Her stomach seemed to turn a somersault in her mid-section. "Oh?"

Dad nodded. His ears glowed bright red. "Yes. Gramma thought this friend and you and I should ... meet."

And Katy understood. Gramma was playing matchmaker!

"Can Annika come too?" Katy blurted the request.

Dad froze for a moment but then gave a quick nod. "Go see if it's all right with her mom."

Katy dashed off. *Please let it be all right! Please! Please!* Between spending more time with Annika and getting ready for Jewel's party, Katy had completely forgotten Dad's comment about her needing a mother. She couldn't believe Gramma Ruthie was acting on Dad's words so quickly. Katy's mother had come from a community in Ohio to marry Dad, but things hadn't worked so well. Would Dad really take a chance on courting another woman from a different community?

Katy came to a halt beside Annika's mom. "Mrs. Gehring, Dad says it's all right if Annika comes to dinner at Gramma Ruthie's today. Can she come?" The words flew out, her heart pounding. If she had to sit at the table and look at the woman who might become her stepmother, she needed the support of a friend. To her great relief, Annika's mother agreed. Katy looped her hand through Annika's elbow. "Stay close. Don't leave my side!"

Annika's face reflected confusion, but Katy didn't have time to explain. When they reached Grampa and Gramma's house, Gramma welcomed the girls with hugs. Then she took Katy's hand and led her over to the woman from church, who stood stirring a pot of corn at Gramma's stove.

"Katy, this is Mrs. Rosemary Graber from Meschke, Kansas. She's a good friend of my cousin Lavinia — you know Lavinia and her husband, Fred. We visited them a few Christmases ago at their farm near Meade. Remember?

Well, Mrs. Graber has been staying with Lavinia for the past several months, and Lavinia thought she would enjoy visiting here."

Why? Did Lavinia get tired of having Mrs. Graber underfoot? Fortunately, Katy's tongue stuck to the roof her mouth, holding the snide remark inside.

Gramma squeezed Katy's hand. "Rosemary, this is my granddaughter Katy—Samuel's girl."

Mrs. Graber smiled and wiped her hands on her apron—one Katy had sewn for Gramma for Christmas last year, she noted. "It's very nice to meet you, Katy."

"Kathleen," Katy corrected.

The woman's eyebrows rose.

"My family calls me Katy, but I prefer Kathleen."

Gramma's eyebrows shot up.

Mrs. Graber smiled and nodded. "Kathleen. Your grandmother speaks of you often and fondly."

Katy looked into the woman's face. She wouldn't call Mrs. Graber beautiful, but she was handsome with a square jaw and strong features. Her eyes—brown on the outer edge of her irises with green at the center—were easily her most appealing feature. What little of her hair Katy could see from beneath the brim of her hat appeared red with strands of silver. She looked nothing like Katy's mother.

Gramma tugged on Katy's hand, and Katy realized she'd been staring silently for several seconds. She cleared her throat. "Thank you." But she didn't say it was nice to meet the woman. She wasn't sure about that yet, and she wouldn't lie.

Gramma introduced Annika to Mrs. Graber, and the pair shook hands. Mrs. Graber said, "I'm glad to meet

Kathleen's best friend. I imagine you girls have lots of fun together."

Annika shrugged, shooting Katy a wide-eyed look of *what should I say?*

Gramma cleared her throat. "Go set the table, girls." She shooed them from the kitchen.

They set the table for six while Gramma's and Mrs. Graber's voices carried from the kitchen. The two women chatted and laughed softly as if they'd been friends for a long time. Katy's hands shook as the placed forks, spoons, and knives beside the plates.

Annika scurried to her side and whispered, "Is it what I think it is? They're trying to match your dad with this lady?"

Katy nodded and whispered back. "Just when I thought things were settling down, Gramma has to go and play matchmaker." She sent a quick glance toward the kitchen doorway. "What do you think of her?"

"I'm not sure. She seems nice — really smiley. But it's hard to tell."

A funny feeling filled Katy's chest — a protective, jealous, uncomfortable feeling she didn't quite understand. She hissed, "Dad and I have been just fine all these years. We don't need anybody else."

Annika shook her head, blowing out a long breath. "Oh, boy ..."

Oh, boy, indeed!

Grampa and Dad came from the living room as Gramma and Mrs. Graber carried out platters and bowls of food. Grampa plopped into his customary seat at the head of the table, and Gramma moved to the foot. Normally Katy would sit beside Annika on one side, but today she darted forward and grabbed Dad's elbow. "Sit by me, Dad."

Grampa Ben offered thanks for the meal and then reached for the platter of pork chops. "You're in for a treat, Rosemary. These chops come from hogs Samuel raises and we butcher ourselves—best meat you'll ever eat." He forked a thick chop onto his plate and passed the platter to Annika.

Gramma picked up the bowl of corn. She smiled brightly at Dad. "Samuel, Rosemary brought this canned sweet corn with her. Comes from her garden back in Meschke. She tells me she cans all sorts of fruits and vegetables every summer."

Katy took the bowl of corn from Gramma. Instead of taking any of the corn swimming in some sort of creamy sauce, she stretched her arms past Dad to thrust the bowl at Grampa. Dad scowled and plucked the bowl from her hands. He put two big spoonfuls on his plate.

"Yes, sir," Grampa said as if agreeing with someone. "Samuel here keeps us all in milk, pork, and beef. Don't know what we'd do without him."

Mrs. Graber smiled shyly at Dad. Dad smiled back shyly, his ears all red.

Katy snatched the bowl of rice from the middle of the table. "We just buy this at the grocery."

Dad bumped Katy with his elbow. She wished she could bump him back. She smacked a spoonful of rice onto her plate and passed the bowl to Dad. Gramma handed her the gravy, and she smothered her rice and pork chop. Mrs. Graber took a small portion of rice and ignored the gravy. For reasons she couldn't explain, Katy felt embarrassed by the hearty portions on her own plate.

Talk fell away while everyone dug into their food. Katy exchanged looks with Annika, her gaze flitting between Mrs. Graber and Dad to be sure they weren't paying too much attention to each other. She knew she was acting childish, but the mere thought of that woman with her father was too much. Just as Katy lifted her fork to put a bite of pork chop in her mouth, Mrs. Graber said, "Kathleen?"

Katy clanked her teeth with the fork.

"Your grandparents tell me you attend the public high school in Salina."

Katy held the bite of pork in her mouth without chewing.

"I would imagine that's been very interesting. What do you like best about high school?"

Everyone stared at Katy, waiting for her to answer. She gave the piece of meat two big chomps and tried to swallow. It caught at the back of her throat. She tried again to swallow, but it wouldn't go down. She grabbed up her glass of water and chugged. The water chased the meat down her esophagus. She put down her glass and released a breath of relief that she hadn't choked.

Mrs. Graber still sat, her fork poised in her hand and her eyes on Katy. Gramma, Grampa, Dad, and Annika also sat motionless. They reminded Katy of a still-life painting from her history book. She gave their picture a title: *Family at Impasse.* She giggled. High-pitched. Hysterical.

Mrs. Graber's eyebrows shot up.

"Katy?" Dad's voice boomed in the quiet room. "Mrs. Graber asked you a question."

"Oh. Yes." Katy traced a curlycue in the gravy in her plate with her fork. She offered what she hoped was an innocent look. "I'm sorry, I've forgotten. What was the question again?"

"Your favorite part of high school . . . ?"

Katy wasn't about to share her joy in attending English class. She flipped her fingers, as if shooing away a fly. "Oh, I couldn't say ..." She ignored Dad's warning frown, lifted a forkful of rice, and chewed with great concentration.

Mrs. Graber smiled sweetly. "Never mind, Kathleen. Go ahead and eat."

Katy bent over her plate and focused on her dinner. How she hoped Mrs. Graber got the message. She didn't want to be friends. And Dad was *not* up for grabs.

That evening, Dad and Katy sat in the living room for their customary time of Bible reading and prayer before retiring. Katy expected Dad to scold her for her behavior at Gramma's dinner table, but he never said a word about the way she'd treated Mrs. Graber. He read a passage from Psalms, his voice deep and soothing and calm. His prayers didn't carry even a hint of irritation with her. She bowed her head and prayed that Dad hadn't fallen for Gramma and Grampa's scheme to match him with the woman who grew and canned her own vegetables. They didn't need a woman around here. They were fine on their own.

"Bed now, Katy-girl," Dad said at the close of his prayer.

"Good-night, Dad."

Katy dressed in her gown and then sat at her desk. She pulled out her journal and recorded the events of the past two days—Jewel's party, Annika putting Caleb in his place, and her time with Annika at the pond that afternoon. She carefully avoided any mention of Mrs. Graber.

Her recording complete, she began idly flipping pages. The journal fell open to the poem she'd written about the leaf. She read it again, frowning a bit. Then slowly, deliberately, she drew a line through the last two lines. With careful strokes, she crafted a different ending.

~~The wind comes stronger, pulling hard . . .~~
~~The last leaf falls upon the yard.~~
Although the wind pulls very hard,
The last leaf clings without regard;
And at the close of winter chill,
Finds its joy in remaining there still.
Joyfully remains there still.

She smiled, closed the book, and turned off her lamp.

"Kathleen, your essay is one of the best I've read in all my years of teaching." Mr. Gorsky folded his arms on the edge of the desk.

Katy couldn't deny the rush of pleasure her teacher's words brought. When he'd asked her to come in before lunch and visit with him, she had worried she'd done something wrong. She stared at her neatly written essay lying on top of the stack of typed papers on his desk. She owned no computer, so her work was always handwritten. Mr. Gorsky never complained. She'd worked long and hard on the assigned topic, *A Recent Epiphany.*

She'd savored the word *epiphany* and its meaning — a leap of understanding. Her deepest thoughts spilled onto the page as she recorded her realization that she could be a public school student while maintaining the standards of her Mennonite faith. The realization hadn't come easily, and writing about it had been harder than writing a poem, but Mr. Gorsky's affirmation verified her hard work had paid off.

He continued, "There's a Young Writers contest sponsored by *Journalistic Pursuits* magazine, and I would like you to enter it. I believe it stands a good chance of winning."

Katy's ears burned red hot. Published in a magazine? "Th-thank you, sir, but I better ask my dad before I say yes."

Mr. Gorsky smiled. "That's fine. The deadline is December one, so don't wait too long, all right?"

"No, sir, I won't." She'd ask Dad the minute he met the bus. Katy started to leave.

"Kathleen?"

She turned back.

The teacher rose and rounded the desk. "Would you also ask your dad for permission to join the yearbook staff? With your writing abilities, you'd be an excellent addition to the staff. You might also consider joining the debate and forensics squads. I'm sure your excellent ability to communicate in written form would extend to communicating verbally."

Katy gulped. Mr. Gorsky's confidence in her abilities put a lump in her throat that refused to be swallowed. She nodded.

"Good. I'll see you on Monday, Kathleen."

Katy stepped into the hallway and leaned against the door for a moment. Her heart pounded. Maybe being published! Writing for the yearbook! Joining the debate team! The thoughts made her giddy. *Don't get carried away. Dad might say no.* Then she followed the thought with a prayer; *God, if You want me to step through these doors, then put a "yes" in Dad's mouth.*

Smiling, she headed to her locker and deposited her backpack. Then she hurried to the cafeteria. Laughter and voices — by now a familiar sound — guided her to the large room. Her lunch period was half over, and only a few kids stood in line at the serving counter. She darted forward and grabbed a tray. The servers scooped a chicken-fried steak patty, mashed potatoes, shriveled peas, and a peach half onto her plate, and she thanked each of them in turn. She added a small carton of milk and then scanned the crowded lunchroom for Shelby and the others.

"Kathleen!" The word carried over the noise. "Over here!"

Katy spotted Shelby waving her arm. An empty seat waited between Shelby and Bridget. Katy scurried over.

"*There* you are," Bridget said, shaking her head. "We thought you got lost."

"Mr. Gorsky needed to talk to me."

Cora giggled. "You in trouble?"

Jewel rolled her eyes. "We're talking about *Kathleen*. As if *she'd* be in trouble ..."

Shelby scooted her chair over a little bit. "We saved you a seat. Sit down."

Katy placed her tray on the table and slipped into the open chair.

Cora leaned forward. "Hey, Kathleen, did you — "

"Hush!" Trisha scowled at the always chattering Cora. "You know Kathleen prays before she eats. Leave her alone for a minute."

Something — something *good* — welled up inside of Katy. She bowed her head to say grace, adding a "Thank

You, Lord," that had nothing to do with food. She whispered, "Amen," and lifted her head.

Picking up her fork, she pointed it at Cora. "Before you say anything else, there's something you should know ..." She glanced around the circle of girls. A smile grew on her face, and she bestowed it by turn on Shelby, Bridget, Cora, Trisha, and even Jewel. "My friends call me Katy."

Share Your Thoughts

With the Author: Your comments will be forwarded to the author when you send them to *zauthor@zondervan.com.*

With Zondervan: Submit your review of this book by writing to *zreview@zondervan.com.*

Free Online Resources at

www.zondervan.com

Zondervan AuthorTracker: Be notified whenever your favorite authors publish new books, go on tour, or post an update about what's happening in their lives.

Daily Bible Verses and Devotions: Enrich your life with daily Bible verses or devotions that help you start every morning focused on God.

Free Email Publications: Sign up for newsletters on fiction, Christian living, church ministry, parenting, and more.

Zondervan Bible Search: Find and compare Bible passages in a variety of translations at www.zondervanbiblesearch.com.

Other Benefits: Register yourself to receive online benefits like coupons and special offers, or to participate in research.

ZONDERVAN® .com